The Mys... ...ival
...stories

Bilingual Press/Editorial Bilingüe

Address:
Bilingual Review/Press
Hispanic Research Center
Arizona State University
Tempe, Arizona 85287
(602) 965-3867

The Mystery of Survival

and other stories

Alicia Gaspar de Alba

Bilingual Press/Editorial Bilingüe
TEMPE, ARIZONA

ISBN 0-927534-32-0 (paper)

Library of Congress Cataloging-in-Publication Data

Gaspar de Alba, Alicia, 1958-
The mystery of survival and other stories / by Alicia Gaspar de Alba.
p. cm.
ISBN 0-927534-32-0 (paper)
1. Mexican American women—Fiction. 2. Mexican Americans—Fiction. I. Title.
PS3557.A8449M97 1993
813'.54—dc20 93-14834
CIP

PRINTED IN THE UNITED STATES OF AMERICA

Cover design by Thomas Detrie

Back cover photo by Deena J. González

Acknowledgments

Partial funding provided by the Arizona Commission on the Arts through appropriations from the Arizona State Legislature; additional funding provided by a grant from the National Endowment for the Arts in Washington, D.C., a Federal agency.

Acknowledgment is made to the following anthologies for stories that were originally published in their pages:

Palabra nueva: Cuentos chicanos (El Paso: Texas Western Press, 1984): "El pavo."
Palabra nueva: Cuentos chicanos II (El Paso: Dos Pasos Editores, 1986): "They're Just Silly Rabbits."
IV Encuentro Nacional de Escritores en la Frontera Norte/1989 (Ciudad Juárez: Centro Editorial Universitario de la Universidad Autónoma de Ciudad Juárez): "Los derechos de la Malinche."
Blue Mesa Review (Albuquerque: Creative Writing Center, University of New Mexico, Spring 1990): "The Prediction."

The religious ceremonies depicted in these stories are fictional; they are specifically *not* appropriations of indigenous spiritual rituals nor representative of any native traditions.

Contents

Author's Preface

These stories evolved over the first seven years of my writing career, from 1982 to 1989. During that time, I moved from El Paso to Juárez to San Miguel de Allende to Iowa City to Boston—a period of tremendous movement and change (which continues) that found expression in the moving lines and fluid boundaries of fiction. My training as a writer is primarily in poetry. Poems are such different creatures from stories. Poems are guests who know just how long to stay. Stories move in, all that extra baggage that never has a place, that crowds you out. You don't know how relieved I am that these stories have finally found a place of their own.

Perhaps the most difficult thing about fiction for me, the "mystery of survival" in the art of fiction, is the continuity, the daily discipline, but also, the equanimity that is necessary to probe and decipher, to connect and forgive. What I love about stories is the flow, the movement of words over the page that is the closest a writer can get to walking on water.

16 October 1992
Santa Barbara

Piñatas of Memory: Alicia Gaspar de Alba's Stories of Survival

Cordelia Candelaria
Arizona State University

Remember the piñatas of your past? If you grew up on the United States side of the Border, the familiar, brightly decorated, candy-filled, papier-mâché figures were staples of birthday parties and other festivities. On the Mexican side, as the sharp-eyed protagonist of "The Piñata Dream" in this collection reminds us, "piñatas used to be used only for Christmas, that's what my grandpa told me, and that's why they were so beautiful and so special, and they were shaped like stars to symbolize the star of Bethlehem." But whether or not your remembered piñata was a traditional plump star with crepe paper streamers curling off each point for Christ's birthday, or a smiling Mickey Mouse twirling from a tree branch for a decidedly secular fiesta, or even a more contemporary Miss Piggy pinned on a college dormitory wall for decoration only, the piñatas of your memory very likely are filled with much more than sweets and dime store toys alone—as they are for many of the characters in these *cuentos*.

This reflection came to me from reading Alicia Gaspar de Alba's fine stories, which are assembled like a loosely woven novel in this, her first short story collection, *The Mystery of Survival and Other Stories*. The "piñatas of memory" are literally drawn in "The Piñata Dream," a *cuento* about a young writer, Mary, whose epiphany grows out of her studied exploration of childhood memory, particularly her recurrent nightmare of "kill[ing] the glass piñata" that haunts her until, with the help of a New Age-like guide, she can explode its symbolism and recover her cultural identity as Xochitl María Espinosa.

Piñatas are also figuratively drawn throughout the collection, which is pointedly epigraphed with the *dicho*, "El pueblo que pierde su memoria pierde su destino." For example, in "Los derechos de La

Malinche," one of two stories written entirely in Spanish, the piñata figure that holds the remembered past is the "amuleto de cristal en forma de pirámide," and in "Estrella González" the piñata's emblem is the old man Joaquín's recollection of the curandera, Estrella, which he shared with his curious grandchildren when he finally "felt brave enough to tell the tale." Ultimately, the book resembles a piñata of words, adorned with parrots, *pavos*, and other symbols from nature and filled with compelling characters, intricately drawn plots, and memories steeped in experience and confronted by a mature writer's startling understanding. From this perspective, the "bat" that opens up the narrative piñata is the reader's engaged sensibility.

The crafter of these tales, Alicia Gaspar de Alba, was born in 1958 in El Paso, Texas, "dropped," she says in her "Abstract of a Life in Progress" in *Three Times a Woman* (Tempe, AZ: Bilingual Review/Press, 1989), "from a two-headed tree of mexicanos . . . the first Chicana fruit of the family" (p. 4). A true *fronteriza,* she grew up near El Paso's Córdoba Bridge and was immersed in the Mexicano/ Tejano ambience of the Border, what she calls "cultural schizophrenia" in her personal essay, "Literary Wetback" (*The Massachusetts Review*, vol. XXIX, no. 2, 1988). The year of her eighth-grade graduation from a private Catholic girls' school, Loretto Academy, also held two other important milestones for her: the death of her grandfather and her first publication (a short story). Between this beginning as a published writer and completion of her master of arts degree in English at the University of Texas at El Paso in 1983, she married her high school boyfriend, came out as a Chicana and then as a lesbian, divorced, and kept writing—mostly poetry but occasionally fiction and essays. In 1985, she entered a doctoral program in American Studies at the University of Iowa, but left that program after nine months and moved to Boston. She lived in Boston's Back Bay for four years, came face to face with racism, taught freshman composition and ESL at that city's University of Massachusetts campus, transcribed children's books into Braille, and began active publishing (e.g., in *Revista Chicano-Riqueña, Imagine: International Poetry Journal, Iowa Journal of Literary Studies, Common Lives/ Lesbian Lives,* etc.). In Boston, she completed *The Mystery of Survival and Other Stories*, which she aptly described in 1989 as "*frontera* folk tales." Now back in the West, living in California with Chicana historian Deena González, she is completing her dissertation in American Studies from the University of New Mexico and learning to negotiate an academic career with a writing life. Despite her lack of time, she continues to write (she is currently working on a novel about Sor Juana Inés de la Cruz and on a second collection of poetry), to give readings, and to assure her writer's destiny by cherishing her private memories and those bequeathed her by family (original and acquired) and culture (Chicana and lesbiana) and by memorializing them in her writing.

This collection plants the first seeds of Gaspar de Alba's fiction in the fruitful soil tilled by such North American writers as Sherwood Anderson, Flannery O'Connor, Toni Morrison, and Estela Portillo Trambley. She shares several of their interests and, in incipient form, some of their techniques. Like Anderson in *Winesburg, Ohio* and O'Connor in her short stories about the South, Gaspar de Alba situates her short fiction in one central locale—the Border, usually between the United States and Mexico, but also the cultural "borders" that separate people throughout America. Also like Anderson and O'Connor, she focuses on the ethical moral choices people make that determine the courses of their lives and ultimate destinies (e.g., the absent father in "The Mystery of Survival," the would-be journalist in "American Citizen, 1921," and Susana the prostitute in "La Mariscal"). Like Morrison and Portillo Trambley, Gaspar de Alba probes the flaws and weaknesses within her ethnoracial roots and, through her characters and their situations, makes fresh discoveries about the very permeable conditions of race, economic class, and gender and sexuality (see especially "El pavo," "The Prediction," and "Facing the Mariachis." This collection also calls to mind such effective contemporary Chicana writers as Ana Castillo, Cherríe Moraga, and Helen Viramontes. Like them Gaspar de Alba has also published poetry extensively, and her project as a writer is focused on dispelling facile stereotypes about Chicanas, sexuality and heterosexism, and Mexican America in its textured diversity.

In describing these *cuentos* as "assembled like a loosely woven novel," I mean to underscore two qualities that I find particularly powerful in this book when read sequentially from page one to the end. First, I was struck by each narrator's and/or protagonist's strong oppositional voice, usually not as obvious political rebels pushing a monolithic ideology—although some of the stories in the first section lack the subtlety of the four titles in "Xochitl's Stories"—but as complex, conflicted individuals struggling to comprehend their places within their cultures, political states, and, philosophically, within the cosmos. Second, the writer's interest in psychological issues and metaphysical questions appears to evolve progressively from story to story in a way that deepens the book's embracing thematics much as a drama's structure of rising action, climax, and denouement unites plot and theme seamlessly. In this regard, I found especially successful the way Gaspar de Alba returns in the final story, "Facing the Mariachis," to several key elements (incest, Xochitl, the curandera Estrella, *canciones*, etc.) introduced in the earlier stories. As a result, and like the conclusion of Sandra Cisneros's *The House on Mango Street*, the collection establishes a writerly authority through its structural coherence. It also offers an ethnopoetic resolution that finds real answers in the deep texture of cultural tradition, personal memory, and subject-defined aesthetics.

When I finished reading these stories in one sitting, their ethnopoetic power reminded me of the first time I met Alicia. We had invited her to read poetry at the University of Colorado's International Women's Week Conference in March 1987, and one of her poems blew me away with its power and beauty. Later published in *Three Times a Woman*, that poem, "Beggar on the Córdoba Bridge," still resonates in the labyrinth of my memory as an elegant inscription of one profound meaning of *mestizaje*, Border consciousness, and poetic vision.

Beggar on the Córdoba Bridge

(50 pesos for a poem)

I want to keep you, old woman.
Knit your bones
in red wool, wear your eye
teeth around my neck—
amulets filled with sage.

You could teach me
the way of the gypsy:
how to dream
in an open field
(cotton or onion)
and let my hair grow long
roots in the mud.

How to take bread or fish
from the mouths of dogs,
travel bridges that are pure light,
tell the fortunes of rats.
From you, I could learn to read
the cracked, brown palm
of the Río Grande.

I want to keep you, old woman.
Weave your crow's feet
into my skin, polish
the black coins of your eyes—
currency of a higher kind.

Just as the poem moves from concrete image and actual experience to the abstract and reverential mystery of metaphor without sacrifice or loss of concretion, so too do these stories of survival. Through their insistence upon healing and wholeness through immersion in, and comprehension of, the plain specifics of everyday life, they capture the magic of fiction in chronicling one woman's life and imagination.

Para mis madres

Teyali Falcón Vargas
Guadalupe Vizcarra Quintero

El pueblo que pierde su memoria
pierde su destino
—dicho mexicano

A people that loses its memory
loses its destiny
—Mexican proverb

Puros Cuentos

The Mystery of Survival

When my mother left me in the Colonia La Gran María, I was ten years old and I hated men. My stepfather had once told me that women were like the earth, and that men could mine them and take anything they wanted. Girls, he said, especially ones like me who talked back and disobeyed, had to be dealt with in a special way. I remember that evening like a deep secret I must never tell. My mother had gone to the orphanage with food and some of my old clothes.

"I'm not a woman," I cried, terrified, staring down at the thing sticking out of his pants.

"You're a bad girl!" he told me, spanking me hard. "Men have to punish bad girls."

He spanked me again and made me take it in my mouth. Later, when my mother came home, he went into the kitchen and told her I could no longer stay in his house.

"He doesn't love you. We can't live here anymore," my mother said as we walked to the plaza. "We're going away. To la frontera. To my cousin Lucía's house."

"Is your cousin Lucía married, Mamá?" I asked.

"She works on the other side. Maybe she can find me a job," she said. She had not heard my question.

In the plaza, we found an empty bench near the kiosko, and Mamá told me to sit with my back to her so that she could rebraid my hair with the new ribbons she'd bought me.

"Why does he do those things to me, Mamá?"

She unwound my hair and combed it out with her fingers. "Remember, hija," she said at length, "the mystery of survival is obedience. If we can obey even the most terrible thing, we will survive it. If we disobey, we will always lose. Remember that. Obey and you will survive. Disobey and you will suffer."

"But it hurts me, sometimes, what he does."

"You *think* you hurt now, hija," she said, starting on the second braid. "Later you'll know that you survived. Later you'll know what real suffering is."

I watched the pigeons and the doves that lined the railing of the kiosko. *Do birds have to obey*? I wondered.

"Come on," Mamá said after she'd finished fixing my hair. "I'll buy you an elote. Do you want one?"

We walked over to the man who was selling boiled corn on the cob. My stomach heaved.

"I'd rather have coconut," I said, and we went to the lady slicing coconut flesh on a cart. "Everything on it," I said to the lady, and I watched her squeeze a lime over some slices in a plastic glass, powder them with red chile, and sprinkle them with salt. The lady handed me the glass, and Mamá paid her from a little bag she wore between her breasts.

"Have you ever been to la frontera?" I asked as we strolled around the plaza eating coconut. Her eyes were shadowed. She did not want to speak.

We left the next morning. The sun had not risen yet, but women were already out sweeping their sidewalks and talking with the men who picked up the trash. I had to carry my clothes and my schoolbooks in a plastic market bag; Mamá lugged an old suitcase. She seemed strangely happy. She was shivering—from the cold, she said—but there was something about her face that I had never seen before. The line between her eyebrows wasn't pleated; her lips weren't pressed together as usual. She had parted her hair differently, and for once, I noticed the soft curve of her jawline, undisturbed by the constant flexing and unflexing of her jaw muscles that was her habit.

"You look beautiful, Mamá," I told her, slipping my free arm around her waist as we walked to the train station. She stroked my cheek, then pressed me tightly to her side.

"My cousin Lucía is very nice," she said. "You're going to be happy, I know."

I narrowed my eyes. Was Mamá planning to leave me with this cousin of hers the way she'd left me with her sister two years ago? Maybe she was going back to live with him. I turned my head and saw him standing on the balcony, tucking his shirt into his open pants.

"Will you stay with me?" I asked, keeping my voice low so that she wouldn't hear the fear in it.

"I *am* with you, hija."

I could smell the starch in her dress and saw that she had worn her new shoes, the ones that she said hurt her when she walked. The market bag felt suddenly too heavy for me. I turned my face toward her body and cried into the dark cloth of her dress.

The bells of Santa Clara tolled for the five-thirty mass, and Mamá turned onto the street that led to the church, digging her mantilla out of her purse.

"Wait for me here," she said outside the entrance, leaving her suitcase beside me. I watched her go down the aisle, genuflect in front of the altar, and turn left where the large picture of the Virgin of Guadalupe hung in its golden frame. She lit a long candle and then knelt down. The smell of incense and wax filtered out to me.

"It's bad luck to stand in the doorway of a church," said an old man who was coming to early mass. I moved over to let him pass and decided to wait for Mamá farther down on the steps. Before leaving the churchyard, we stopped at the fountain where Mamá tossed an American coin into the water. She bought me five bags of pumpkin seeds from a man with no legs.

"We have to hurry," she said. "The train leaves in twenty minutes, and we still don't have our tickets."

In the pink and lavender light of the sunrise, the city looked different to me—I noticed the arches of the old market, the potted poinsettias on the balconies of the post office and the prison, the bright skirts of the Indian women who were peeling prickly pears outside the train station. Inside, two boys wanted to carry our things. Mamá gave them some pesos, and they ran off.

"Stay close to me," Mamá said as we stood in line to get our tickets to Ciudad Juárez.

We pulled out of Querétaro just as the big smelter sounded the morning horn. My stepfather would be leaving the house with his hard hat and the lonchera Mamá had prepared for him last night. Yesterday at this hour, I was eating my breakfast and trying to memorize the paragraph in my biology book that I had to recite at school. Mamá was listening to the radio as she finished ironing my uniform. Sitting on the black seat of the moving train, I realized that the same thing that happened to snakes could happen to people.

Just outside the city limits of Querétaro, the train passed a long, whitewashed wall painted with the election messages of the PRI and PAN, and beside them, a proverb in green letters: EL PUEBLO QUE PIERDE SU MEMORIA PIERDE SU DESTINO. I asked Mamá what it meant.

"I don't know," she said. "Mexican proverbs don't mean anything anymore."

I looked out the window and tried to memorize the shape of the Cerro de las Campanas, the Hill of Bells, where a bronze Benito Juárez stood twenty meters into the sky. The same hill where Maximilian had once faced the firing squad.

Thirty-six hours later, we were stepping onto the platform of the station in Ciudad Juárez, where we were instantly swallowed into a crowd. Mamá held me by the back of the neck as she tried to maneuver us through all those bodies. Finally outside, we caught a taxi, and Mamá told the driver the name of the colonia we wanted to go to. The man shook his head and told us that taxis didn't go into the colonias. For that, we would have to take a "rutera," and he pointed to a white van that was just leaving the station.

"Take the one that says 'colonias,' " the man called behind us as we stepped out. "And get ready for the stink!"

The rutera stuffed thirty of us inside, even though the sign painted on the door said there was room for only eighteen passengers. I looked out the grimy window and tried to breathe. Mamá did not tell me we were coming to a place where people did not wash, a place that had beggars on every corner and more trash than trees. The rutera zigzagged through the lines of traffic and crossed the railroad tracks just before a cargo train whistled by. Mamá asked the woman bending over her if the driver was crazy.

"That's the way they are," the woman said. "Are you from the south?"

"From Querétaro," Mamá said. "My daughter and I are looking for the colonia La Gran María."

"La Gran María?" the woman repeated. I turned and saw the woman shaking her head as if she had just heard bad news. "That's the last stop," she said.

The rutera screeched to a halt, and the woman and another passenger squeezed out. Ahead of us I could see bare, brown hills and unpaved streets.

"I don't like it here," I told Mamá.

"You didn't like it at home, either," she said.

I gazed out the window again at the whirls of dust, the flat adobe houses caked with crumbling paint, the barefoot babies, the dry hills. We were the last ones in the rutera, and I noticed that the driver was slowing down, that the roads had more potholes, that the houses were now made of sticks and cardboard. I looked up at Mamá, our eyes meeting, holding, letting go.

"La Gran María!" the driver barked, and we had barely lifted Mamá's suitcase from the van before the rutera jerked into reverse and disappeared behind a cloud of black fumes.

"Thank God we're off that thing," Mamá said, smoothing the wrinkles from the back of her dress. "Look at your face! It's all smeared." She opened her purse and rummaged through it. Behind her, the tin shacks of the colonia La Gran María reflected rusty sunlight. A group of kids that had been playing kick the can in the road came up and watched us.

"Here it is," Mamá said. She took out her handkerchief, wet a tip of it with her tongue, and started cleaning my face.

A rat ran out of the Abarrotes store, chased by a woman with a broom.

"This is the ugliest place I've ever seen," I said.

"Ugly is in your soul," she answered. "If your soul is clean, nothing around you can ever be ugly."

"Then why are you taking so long to turn around?" I said. She slapped me, then continued wiping my face.

"You don't speak to your mother that way," she said. The kids laughed. "Besides, this is only temporary." She put the handkerchief away and turned around to face the colonia. "When I get a job, we'll—" She drew her breath. "—we'll move," she said.

I picked up the market bag and walked off.

"Where are you going?" she called behind me. "You don't even know where you're going."

Neither do you, I told her silently, pressing the tears out of my eyes with the heel of my free hand. Past the last row of shacks, I could see a cottonwood, and below it, the sparse, green bank of a narrow river. Two wide highways, separated by a stretch of desert, shimmered on the other side of the river. Beyond the highways, on a landscaped hill, stood a pair of tall, white buildings and a parking lot with rows of cars.

"There she is!" Mamá cried behind me, and then, louder,

"Lucía!" Mamá dropped her suitcase and ran towards the other woman, her plump arms swinging from side to side. The other woman, taller and younger than Mamá, with short black hair and a great mole on the side of her face, opened her arms and hugged my mother.

"Ven acá," Mamá called me, waving me over with one arm while she kept her other arm around her cousin's shoulder. I sucked my cheeks in and came closer, and the woman named Lucía bent down to study my face. She had large, owl-like eyes that seemed to change from brown to yellow right in front of me.

"At last I meet my only niece," she said, holding out her hand. I shook it, but it felt more like having my hand swallowed, like a big fish gulping down a little fish. "Are you hungry?" she asked.

I looked at Mamá and Mamá nodded.

"No," I said. "I'm thirsty."

"Who isn't?" Lucía said, standing up again and reaching for my market bag. "Everything is thirsty in the desert." She took Mamá's suitcase as well.

"She's being a Mrs. Contreras right now," Mama told Lucía. "If I say good, she'll say bad. If I say food, she'll say water."

I stayed behind them as we walked in the direction of one of the shacks. Suddenly, a white dog bounded out from behind a heap of old tires. Mamá screamed. Lucía whistled sharply, and the dog slowed down.

"This is Sancho," Lucía said when the dog was beside me, sniffing my knees. "Don't be afraid of him. He's a good friend."

I had never touched a white dog before, and his fur felt strangely soft, strangely clean in this dusty place. He stood there patiently while I petted his back and scratched between his pink-tipped ears.

"Don't worry," Lucía told Mamá as they moved on, "my father whipped all the wildness out of him."

Her father? I thought. *Does Mamá's cousin Lucía have a man in her house?* The mask of my stepfather's face fell over the dog's head. Eyes bloodshot. Teeth bared. *You're a bad girl! Men have to punish bad girls. Get the devil out of them. Clean the devil out with this. Swallow it! Swallow it!*

Sharp needles were pushing into my head. My mouth tasted of blood and vomit. Far away, I heard my mother's voice. "She hardly ate on the train," she was saying.

I heard the sound of swishing water, then something sticky and wet covered my forehead. It smelled of melon.

"She's waking up," said another voice, closer. My eyes cracked open.

"Also, maybe it was the heat." Mamá sounded old. I heard the squeaking of bedsprings, and then I was helped to sit up, my head resting on an unknown hand. The wet thing on my forehead fell off, and I saw that it was a cantaloupe rind.

"Drink this, hija." Hot liquid touched my lips. The smell of chicken broth woke me completely. I was lying on a box spring in a room with no windows, the afternoon light slicing in through the cracks in the roof and walls. A cot with a thin mattress and a pillow stood in a corner. Two crates pushed up against a table served as chairs. On another crate, an altar had been assembled, crowded with the framed pictures of saints, votive candles, a jar of dark liquid, and a tin cup with feathers in it. The glow of the candles flickered on the dirt floor.

I was gulping the broth down more quickly than Mamá could spoon it out of the bowl, and Lucía told me that I was going to make myself sick again if I ate so fast.

"I'm hungry," I told her, remembering suddenly that she had a man in her house, a man who probably slept in that cot over there in this one-room hovel. I pulled away from Lucía and told Mamá that I didn't want to stay here, that I was afraid that the man in this house would do what the other man had done.

Mamá stopped feeding me, her face slowly darkening to a deep red. "Excuse me," she said to her cousin, gesturing with her head that she wanted her to leave us alone. Quietly, Lucía left, taking the half-finished bowl of soup with her. When she had gone, and the sheet flapped over the doorway again, Mamá turned to me and slapped me hard.

"You must never talk about that!" she hissed. "If you do, La Llorona will come for you. She'll drag you to the river and drown you."

I bent my head to one side, eyes narrowed. "That's not true," I said.

"You'll see," she said. "When you wake up one night and hear her calling you from the window, you'll see if it's true or not."

"She doesn't know my name," I said, tracing the lines in my skirt. "And there aren't any windows, anyway! That's just a cuento!"

"She knows all the Mexican children. I've told you that." She paused for a moment, and her eyes flattened like the ears of an angry cat. "She was there when you were born!"

The look in her eyes made me wet my pants. I knew it would show on my skirt if I got up.

"I'm not afraid," I told her calmly, lying back down. I covered myself with the threadbare sheet and pretended to sleep. She stayed beside me a long time afterwards, mumbling to herself—that same monotonous sound that meant she was praying. Then, she bent over me and made the sign of the cross over my face, pressing her thumb to my mouth for the *Amen*.

"Mamá?" I whispered. "Do you love him more than me?"

She stroked my back. "How can you ask me that?" she said. "I didn't mean to hit you so hard. You embarrassed me in front of Lucía."

"How long do we have to stay here?" I said.

She did not answer right away. Her hand kept stroking me, and I could feel the numbness of sleep spreading down my spine. Finally, she spoke. "I'm going to try to cross the river tonight," she said. "Lucía tells me they are hiring at the university. I'll be close by. Right across the river in those buildings we saw."

"That's a university?" I said, my eyes sinking deeper and deeper into sleep.

"I'll take you to the movies every Sunday, just like I used to in Querétaro. And I'll bring you story books in English; Doña Inés can teach you how to read them. By the time you're fifteen, I'll have my green card, and we can live on the other side."

"Who's Doña Inés?" I was barely awake.

She bent over me again and kissed my cheek. "Go to sleep. Lucía will tell you all about Doña Inés later." She kissed me two more times, then got up and was gone.

A dry breeze swirled into the room. A branch rattled against the side of the shack. The wet spot had started to sting, and I thought it would be a good idea to take off my skirt and let it dry in the breeze, but I was too numb to move. I closed my eyes and was already asleep when I heard someone coming into the room. For one terrible instant, I thought it was Lucía's father. I clenched my fists and my eyes, but then something cold pressed against the back of my neck. It was only Sancho sniffing at this stranger in his house. I heard him flop down beside the bed, a deep yawn coming from his mouth. *Good friend*, I thought over and over.

I must have slept for over two hours because when I awoke, a kerosene lamp had been lit on the table, and everything in the room looked huge with shadow. I sat up suddenly, for a moment not knowing where I was. Then I noticed that Mamá's suitcase was open and her clothes were gone, and I jumped out of the tangled bedsheet and tore outside.

Lucía and an old man were sitting on tires before a stove made with bricks and a piece of tin. It was nearly dusk. The air smelled of woodsmoke and hot corn. Lucía stood up as I approached. "Papá, here she is," she said to him.

The old man stared at the tortillas warming on the tin and nodded his head. Beside him, Sancho thumped his tail on the dirt. Mamá was not there.

"Everybody calls my father Tito," Lucía said.

"Where's my mother?" I asked, nearly spitting the words at her.

"She had to cross *tonight*," Lucía explained, pointing down in the direction of the river. "She wanted to let you rest. She said to tell you to be strong and to send her good luck so that she gets across safely."

"When is she coming back?" I said.

The old man raised his face to look at me, and I saw that he was ancient, and that his eyes were buried in cataracts. The fear of Lucía's father slipped out of me like a gas.

"She will stay there until she has enough money to come and get you," he said. "Until then, Lucía will take care of you."

A fist suddenly formed in my throat. I could not see the river, only the headlights of the cars on the two highways and the bright windows of the university where Mamá had said she would be working. I imagined standing on the riverbank, looking up, trying to find Mamá's face in one of those windows. I remembered the way I had once looked for the face of Benito Juárez, the statue on the Hill of Bells that stretched so high above Querétaro, its face sometimes hidden in the clouds.

"Vamos," Lucía said, picking up an old flashlight and wrapping a few tortillas in a frayed cloth. "Let's go take these to Doña Inés. She's waiting to meet you."

I followed her out to the road, past other shacks and other makeshift stoves, and felt the eyes of the colonia following me. On the way, a harelipped girl about my age joined us.

"Hola, Lucy," the girl said to Lucía.

"Hola, Guillermina," Lucía said.

The girl grinned at me. I grinned back.

"Doña Inés is our teacher," said Lucía. "She taught Guillermina how to make paper out of rags. She knows English, too."

"Where does she live?" I asked.

"Up here in her school," said Lucía, and we climbed up a steep alley that smelled of wet earth. At the top stood an adobe house surrounded by sunflowers. On a wooden sign nailed to a stake in front of the house, it said: ESCUELA LA GRAN MARIA.

El pavo

Es una mañana de pájaros, nubes, caras en las nubes, silencio. Gabriela se mece en la hamaca a un lado de la casa, chupando un tamarindo. Su abuelo le anda buscando por todas partes, pero él ya no recuerda exactamente qué busca. Abre los gabinetes de la cocina, el horno, se asoma debajo de la mesa, pero es que trae a Pepe en la mente.

—Ese muchacho me va a matar— se dice, rascándose el mechón de canas en la frente. —¡Y esa maldita mocosa también!

Sus hombros caen como un paraguas sobre su pecho. La camiseta está manchada del sudor de cuatro días pero él ya no se fija en esas cosas. Aprieta las manos nudosas y sus dedos rechinan como la madera del piso que había obsesionado a su esposa. Se limpia los ojos con su pañuelo, recordando a aquella mujer tan fuerte, arrodillada, tallando y tallando hasta sacarle la última gota de vida a esa madera. "Me tengo que ver, viejo, si no ni pa' qué perder el tiempo". El viejo se chupa los dientes y por mero le escupe al machimbre, pero se detiene al oír voces en el jardín.

—Ahí anda esa condenada chavala— exclama, agarrando la escoba detrás de la estufa al salir. Se para en el porche, una mano a la cintura, la otra estrujando la escoba.

—Oye tú, chirota, ¿que no te dije que te pusieras a barrer?

Gabriela, parada de manos frente a Pepe, le grita:

—Ahí voy, Grandpa. Le 'stoy enseñando a mi daddy un cartwheel.

Se echa la maroma con las piernas abiertas y la blusa se le sube hasta el cuello, descubriéndole el pecho pálido y huesudo.

—'Hora sí— grita el viejo, casi tropezándose al bajar los escalones —'hora sí me la pagas, pocha desvergonzada ésta . . .

Se empieza a quitar el cinturón y la niña sale corriendo por la calle. Pepe, con unos lentes de sol que lo hacen verse como Eric Estrada de "Chips", se acerca al viejo y le entrega un cartón de Pall Malls.

—¿Cómo está, 'apá?— le pregunta en voz alta.

—Pos, ¿cómo voy a estar?— contesta el viejo, tomando el cartón de cigarros e inspeccionándolo para ver si está abierto.

—Aquí con tu hija que no hace caso. Tres veces le he dicho que barra, pero cómo . . . si anda volada con el güerillo ese.

Pepe se quita los lentes y suspira profundamente.

—¡Ay, 'apá! Usted y sus cosas . . . Nomás porque 'amá . . .

—Tú cállate— le interrumpe el viejo, los labios estirados sobre sus encías moradas. —Tú qué sabes, cabrón— se da la vuelta y avienta la escoba a la tierra.

Pepe mueve la cabeza, haciendo un puño con la mano izquierda, mirando a esa espalda enrojecida por el sol, la camiseta gris, los pantalones sin dobladillo. Se encoge de hombros y va y abre la puerta de atrás de su pick-up.

—¡Gaby!— le grita a su hija que anda jugando a las escondidas con un gato. —Andale, ayúdame con estas bolsas.

—¿Qué me comprastes, Daddy? ¿Los pencils pa' la escuela?— pregunta ella jadeante, con los ojos saltándole como pájaros negros. Pepe no contesta. Le da la bolsa del pan y los huevos y recoge las otras dos. Camina muy despacio, mientras Gabriela hace una mamaleche imaginaria hacia la puerta, llevando la bolsa como muñeca de trapo en la mano.

—No se te vaya a caer, ¿eh?

—No Daddy, yo sé cómo. You know what?

—Habla español, hija, tu abuelo te va a pegar.

Gabriela se detiene en sus brincos y voltea la cara hacia su padre:

—¿Por qué tengo que hablar 'spañol? This is a free country.

Pepe se agacha en cuclillas y baja la voz:

—Free or not, young lady, you talk Spanish in this house. It's his house, ¿me entiendes?

La niña empieza a saltar de nuevo.

—Yes, Daddy, I mean, sí, papi.

Pepe se levanta escupiendo un chorro de tabaco en la banqueta. Sigue caminando, los hoyuelos a cada lado de su boca marcados por su sonrisa apretada.

Cuando entra Gabriela a la casa, el abuelo está sentado en su sillón preferido fumándose un cigarro. Ni ve que su nieta anda con las rodillas raspadas, ni que trae la falda rota. Ni ve a Pepe con sus dos bolsas rebosando de mandado. El humo lo envuelve como una red y sus ojos verdes apenas se ven abiertos. Pepe quiere ir a moverlo pero sabe que ahorita es mejor dejarlo. Mejor que siga con sus recuerdos. Baja las bolsas a la mesa y le hace un gesto a Gabriela para que no hable. La niña se encoge de hombros, haciéndole como que no lo vio, y empieza a sacar las cosas para acomodarlas en los gabinetes:

—C & H Sugar, Mead's Fine Bread, Kellogg's Corn Flakes, Hills Bro . . .

—¡Sshh!— dice Pepe mientras dobla las bolsas.

—Where's my pencils?— dice ella en voz baja y enronquecida.

Pepe arruga la frente y le alza la mano.

—¡Sshh!

La niña hace pucheros y se deja caer al piso pero su padre no le pone atención al berrinche. Salta por encima de ella y le empieza a quitar el papel de aluminio al pavo que le compró a su comadre. "Mire, compa, éste se lo dejo en quince bolas", le dijo ella, sonriéndole como piñata de Navidad, "está bien pechugón". Pepe le da dos manazos al pechugón, tocándole la pierna a su hija con la bota, pero Gabriela no voltea. Pepe levanta el pavo y lo lleva al refrigerador, arrullándolo contra su pecho. Gabriela se asoma por debajo de las piernas de su padre, y al ver el Butterball, pega un gritito de felicidad. Mañana es Thanksgiving y su papi le prometió que iban a tener una fiesta como las que hacía su 'buelita. A ella le va a tocar quebrar los piñones y las almendras con la piedrita del molcajete. No se ha dado cuenta de que su padre no compró ni piñones, ni almendras, ni nada de lo que le ponía su abuela al relleno. Ahorita nada más se imagina sus bolsas llenas de nueces y el olor de las manzanas cociéndose en la panza del pavo. Se levanta del piso y le da un abrazo a su padre que está de rodillas frente al refrigerador.

—Gracias, Daddy— le dice en el oído.

Pepe inclina la cabeza hacia la de su hija y le rodea la cinturita con un brazo.

—¿Ya hicistes la tarea?

Gabriela mueve la cabeza y lo ve por debajo de sus cejas.

—¿Qué tienes que hacer?

—Spelling y penmenchip.

—Bueno, pos apúrate pa' que no la tengas que hacer el Saturday. You know the rules.

—Ay, Daddy, this is a vacation.

—Qué vacation ni que nada. Siempre haces lo mismo y por eso te castiga tu abuelo. Andale, ponte a hacerla.

—Oh Kay— murmura la niña, desprendiéndose del brazo de Pepe. Sale de la cocina lentamente, arrastrando los pies sobre la madera. Sus tenis hacen un chillido que retumba en el silencio de la casa. Un chillido que retumba en los recuerdos del abuelo.

—¡Ya párale!— le grita el viejo de repente. Gabriela se estremece del susto y sale corriendo al jardín. Pepe nada más aprieta las quijadas pero sigue arreglando y desarreglando las cosas en el refrigerador. Hay algo que huele mal y tiene que destapar todos los sartenes y las ollas para ver qué es. Al fin encuentra un plato con algo verdoso refundido en el cajón de las verduras.

—¡Qué asco!— dice, haciendo muecas.

—¿Qué haces, hijo?— pregunta el viejo desde el otro cuarto.

—Nada, 'apá— contesta Pepe como acostumbra. No sabe cómo le va a decir lo del pavo. El viejo ya no quiere cenas ni fiestas. Ahora hasta la gente le molesta.

—Oiga, 'apá, aquí le manda Esperanza— dice Pepe después de un rato, y se muerde la línea delgada de su bigote.

—¿'Hora qué quiere?— contesta el viejo, echando un gargajo al bote de la basura. —Siempre que manda una cosa esa mujer ha de querer algo.

—Pos quién sabe— dice Pepe con la sangre pulsándole en las sienes al oír que el viejo se levanta del sillón.

—Siempre manda algo con cola. Siempre . . .—va diciendo el viejo, acercándose a la cocina. Pepe oye los pasos lentos y pesados en la madera, y por un instante se siente como un niño malcriado, allí hincado en frente de la hielera con las tortillas regadas por el piso y el pavo como una niña desnuda entre la leche y el six-pack de Coors.

—¿Qué es eso?— La voz del viejo suena dura, acabada.

—Pos dice mi comadre que aquí le manda este pavo.

—¡Qué pavo, ni qué la chingada!— explota el viejo. —¿Que no sabe que todavía estamos de luto? ¿O no le dijiste?

Pepe se pone de pie.

—Ay, 'apá, usted sabe cómo es Esperanza; pa' todo se siente.

—Y a mí qué me importa si se siente o no se siente.

Se miran el uno al otro, los ojos de Pepe moviéndose de lado a lado sobre la cara desértica de su padre, buscando una huella de ternura entre esas barbas que le brotan como grises espinas de la piel.

—¿Pos qué esperas?— dice el viejo al fin.

—¿Qué espero para qué?— Pepe quiere escupir. Siente que el tabaco ya se le pudrió en la boca.

—No te hagas pendejo y llévate eso de aquí. Y dile a esa mujer que no se meta en mi vida.

El viejo da media vuelta, pero Pepe lo detiene del brazo.

Ninguno de los dos se da cuenta que Gabriela los está oyendo desde afuera. Balanceada en unas cajas de herramienta que están debajo de la ventana de la cocina, ella puede oír todo perfectamente. Piensa que se debe de poner a barrer para que ya no esté tan enojado su abuelo, y así su papi puede ir por la tía Ramona para que venga a lavar la ropa. No es su tía de verdad, pero Gabriela la quiere mucho porque siempre le anda trayendo cositas que se encuentra en la calle. Una vez le trajo un billete de cinco pesos y le dijo que lo cuidara mucho porque de esos ya no había. Se le ocurre darle ese billete a su abuelo para que se contente. Cruza los dedos para hacer *kinkis* con las dos manos. Estira el cuello y se asoma por la ventana.

—Mira, mira, ya te me pusiste muy bravito— dice el viejo.

—Usted es el que me hace ponerme así, 'apá. Nunca entiende las cosas.

Le suelta el brazo y va a escupir al sink.

—¿Qué quieres que entienda, cabrón?— grita el viejo, arrimándose a Pepe y apuntándole un dedo a la cara. —No, si tú me quieres matar. Te gusta de corazón ponerme así. Siempre queriendo ser tan diferente, tan ambicioso. Ya te crees muy gringo, ¿verdad? Desde que te metiste al colegio ese, ya no respetas, ya no te importan las costumbres y ni tu madre te importa. Nomás lo tuyo, lo tuyo todo el tiempo.

El abuelo empieza a picarle el hombro con el dedo.

—¿Qué quieres? ¿Que me muera de coraje, mientras que tú estás con tus fiestecitas?

Pepe rechina los dientes, su respiración entrecortada, los puños apretados, pero sabe que se tiene que controlar o si no, va a perder como siempre.

—¿Cuáles fiestecitas, oiga? Lo único que quiero es hacerle una cena a la niña. ¿Qué tiene eso de malo?— Se le quiebra la voz al final y casi se quiere dar un tiro.

El viejo no contesta por el momento. Anda ayudándole a su mujer a escoger el pavo más grandote de la tienda. "Somos muchos, viejo, nadie se va a llenar con ése". Al fin dice:

—Se pusieron de acuerdo, ¿verdad?— pero sus ojos están teñidos de dolor.

Pepe agacha la cabeza. No puede verlo así, no puede contra sus lágrimas.

Gabriela no sabe por qué de repente le arden los ojos ni por qué siente como si se hubiera tragado una canica. Algo dentro de ella le dice que su papi va a devolver el turkey. Como chapulín, salta de las cajas y corre por la escoba que todavía está donde la tiró su abuelo.

—Please, Baby Jesus— dice ella entre dientes —please don't let him take it.

Mira hacia el cielo y cree ver la cara de su 'buelita entre las nubes: "Dígale que sí, Grandma, please". Sube al porche y empieza a barrer desesperadamente, su cuerpo girando como trompo. Levanta olas de polvo a su alrededor y luego luego le da comezón y le sale agua de la nariz. Puede oír que ellos todavía están discutiendo en la cocina, pero ya no quiere escuchar qué dicen. Está rezando así como le enseñó su maestra de catecismo: "Please, Baby Jesus; please Holy Father".

—Pos, ¿qué estás haciendo, niña?

Brinca al oír la pregunta de su padre. Para de barrer, y las oleadas de tierra se vuelven a asentar sobre las tablas chuecas del porche. No quiere alzar la cabeza, no quiere ver la bolsa de papel que trae su papi en los brazos. En voz bajita, dice: —"Thanks a lot, Jesus— después se quiere comer la lengua. Su maestra le dijo que nunca debía reprocharle nada al niño Dios porque él sabe lo que hace, pero de todos modos tiene mucho coraje y le duele la panza.

—Vente— le dice Pepe al pasar. —Vamos con Ramona.

La niña se le queda viendo sin entender por qué camina su papi tan aprisa, sus piernas le trabajan como tijeras gigantes. Voltea hacia la casa y ve a su abuelo parado en la puerta con un brazo contra el umbral.

—¿'Onde va mi daddy?— le pregunta, su labio de abajo le tiembla, pero su mirada se mantiene fija, rebelde.

El abuelo no la ve bien hasta ese momento. Una trenza más arriba que la otra, la nariz chorreada, piernas zambas, las manos en la cintura exactamente como se las ponía su vieja con la escoba recargada en el pecho. —'Ta bueno— murmura el viejo, mostrando sus encías, sus ojos hundidos en un mundo de silencio, en una mujer dura, demasiado dura, pero siempre buena y generosa, sin rencores ni reproches. —'Ta bueno, vieja.

La niña frunce las cejas. No entiende qué trae su abuelo ahora con esa sonrisilla. Su papi ya se va con el pavo y no van a tener Thanksgiving, y aquí el viejo está muy contento. De repente, empieza a llorar y a patalear de pura desesperación. Quiere gritarle a su padre que se espere y a su abuelo que ya no se ría. Quiere gritarle hasta a las nubes.

—Cálmate, hija, cálmate— le dice una voz extraña, pero cuando abre los ojos nada más ve a su abuelo deteniéndola de los hombros.

—¿Qué le pasó, 'apá? ¿Qué tiene?— grita Pepe muy asustado.

Brinca al porche sin pisar uno solo de los escalones. La niña voltea a verlo, las lágrimas aún rayándole la cara, y apenas se le oye cuando dice:

—I'm sorry, Daddy . . .

El abuelo se endereza y le truenan unos huesos de la columna. —Ya 'stás muy fregado, Elías— dice en esa misma voz desconocida. —No sé ni pa' qué te pones a pelear—. Se mete a la casa, jorobado, sus piernas y sus brazos tiesos como el ocotillo que anda por el desierto. Sus pasos se mezclan al machimbre y ni Pepe ni Gabriela pueden oír el astillar de aquella madera.

American Citizen, 1921

Alberto Morales looked in the plate glass windows of *The El Paso Herald* and saw that his hat was crooked again. He straightened it, mumbling to himself that he couldn't touch his hat during the interview. He would lay it on his lap after shaking the man's hand firmly and being asked to take a seat. He would slide his hands under his thighs as he answered the man's questions, sitting straight and sure of himself and never looking down at his hat.

These had been his wife's instructions. It was she who had convinced him to come. *You're an American,* she'd said. *You have a right to apply for any job you want. Here, put on your shirt. See how nice I starched it for you? Just remember to keep your hands off your hat, Albert. Sit on them if you have to. And don't worry! You're an American citizen. You can be anything you want.*

When Rosemary spoke to him like that, Alberto could almost feel the brown draining out of his skin, could almost imagine that his father was a conductor for the Southern Pacific instead of a worker who laid the track for it, and that his mother had never borrowed money from the principal of his school. Alberto could see his daughters growing up without fear or shame, nobody pitying them, nobody laughing at their accents, nobody denying them a library card or a high school diploma.

He straightened his hat again, wiped around his mouth with the handkerchief Rosemary had made for him, and walked in.

"I would like an application, please," he told the receptionist in the front office.

The receptionist looked surprised. She told him to go out and wait in the foyer while she got her super. Alberto did not even have time to sit down before the receptionist, followed by a redheaded man in funny glasses, joined him in the foyer.

"Now, what exactly is it that you want?" the man asked. "Thank you, Miss Lind," he said to the receptionist. The young woman looked over her shoulder at Alberto just before stepping back into her office.

"I've come to apply for the job," Alberto said, burying his hands in his trouser pockets. "I read the advertisement—"

"You mean the *reporter* position?" The man pinched off his glasses and stared at Alberto with bulging eyes. "You're . . . why, you're Mexicano, aren't you?"

Alberto took out his right hand and held it in front of the man. "Albert Morales," he said, waiting for the man to notice his hand. "From the graduating class of '17, El Paso High. I'm an American citizen."

The man shook the tips of Alberto's fingers, the frown on his face telling Alberto that he didn't believe him.

"Can I get an application?" Alberto said.

"Well," the man said, scratching his head with his glasses, "just a minute. Let me see what the boss has to say. Just a minute."

The man disappeared behind the glass door. Alberto unfolded his handkerchief again and wiped his whole face. He could smell his nerves stinking up his armpits.

You've got to stop thinking of yourself as a peon, Albert, Rosemary had said. *You have talent. Remember what Miss Foster said. If you put your mind to it, you could be a writer. Show 'em your stories, Albert. The ones with Miss Foster's comments.*

Alberto touched the envelope curled in his coat pocket.

Besides, Rosemary had reminded him, *the* Herald *stands up for people like you. You remember that article last week about how the mayor should clean up the barrios, how unfair it is to let people live in those conditions.*

That doesn't mean they want people like me writing their articles, Alberto had told her.

Well, you just tell 'em to practice what they preach, then! They want people to be fair to Mexicans, let them *set the example. Go on, Albert! You're a high school graduate. You're no ditchdigger. My dad would give us that property in Five Points if you got a real job.*

That's not all he wants me to do, Alberto had said. *And I already told you, I'm not going to become a Mormon.*

He didn't say you had *to convert for him to give us the land. But he won't do it unless you get a decent job. It's half an acre, Albert.*

"Would you follow me, please?" Miss Lind was calling him from the doorway. Alberto's knees bounced a little as he followed her into the clatter of typewriters and the bittersweet smell of old coffee.

"All the way down the aisle and to the left. You'll see Mr. Gaines," she told him.

Alberto felt his hand fidgeting with his hat again, and he took it off as he walked to where Miss Lind had pointed. The noise of the typewriters died down. He knew that every eye in the place was glued to the color of his skin. Alberto did not look around. *Tell 'em to practice what they preach*, he heard again, but he felt like a coyote sneaking through somebody's backyard.

"Here he is. Come on in, muchacho," said Gaines. "Say hello to Mr. Corbitt, editor-in-chief. Sir, this muchacho wants to be a reporter."

Mr. Corbitt was fat and bald. His shirt was open at the collar, and his T-shirt and fingers were stained with ink. "You say you graduated from El Paso High School?" Corbitt spoke with a twang.

"Albert Morales," said Alberto, sticking his hand out, "from the graduating class of—"

"You got your diploma with you?" Corbitt interrupted.

Alberto didn't know what to do with his hat. He stuffed it under his arm and then took out the envelope that held his diploma and stories. "Right here, sir." He slipped the parchment out of the envelope and presented it to Corbitt. "My brother joined the Army, so I'm the one that got to finish high school."

Corbitt scrutinized the diploma. "How do I know this is yours?" he said. "Where's your birth certificate?"

"Birth certificate?" Alberto echoed. "My mother has that, sir. But I could go get it right now and be back in half an hour. If you need to see my writing, I do have these stories from my senior English class." Alberto offered the envelope to Corbitt. "The teacher said that I . . ." He swallowed the spit that had suddenly turned to salt in his throat. ". . . that I had talent. That I could be a writer someday."

"Where does your mother live?" Corbitt asked. "Chihuahuita?"

Alberto nodded. Corbitt looked at Gaines, ignoring Alberto's envelope. Alberto put the stories away, took his hat from under his arm, and punched it back into shape. Why didn't he have the guts to talk to them the way Rosemary would? He was the man of the family, but Rosemary was the one who knew herself. Knew that she didn't want to be called Mexican American, ever. Even though her mother was Mexican, her father and her skin were white, and that's why she would have insisted Corbitt read those stories. She would have read them herself, out loud, so that both Corbitt and Gaines could hear the talent that had written those words. Alberto didn't have Rosemary's advantages, and he didn't really want them, either. But Rosemary wanted the property that her father had offered, and Alberto had promised that he would try.

"Well, Mr. Moralees," the fat man started, "the problem is that that reporter position is filled. We hired a man just an hour ago."

Alberto shrugged. He started to put his hat on, but Gaines held up a hand to stop him.

"I don't think the chief is finished," Gaines said.

Alberto spun the hat by the brim and looked back at Corbitt.

"But we do have an opening for an office boy—"

"Office *assistant*," Gaines put in.

"Yes, an office assistant," said Corbitt. "Something along your line of experience."

"If you play your cards right," Gaines stepped in again, "you might even get to help the reporters out. You do any typing?"

Alberto shook his head. Inside, Rosemary was screaming: *I starched your shirt so that you could get hired as a janitor?*

"Mr. Moralees?"

Alberto blinked back his humiliation. "Excuse me?" he said.

"Mr. Corbitt was saying you might be able to do some research for the reporters."

"In your barrio, especially," added the fat man. "The *Herald* needs an anchor in the barrio, but your people don't trust us. They won't give us any information."

"I don't live in Chihuahuita anymore," said Alberto. "We have an apartment near St. Patrick's."

"Of course you do!" said Gaines. "Mr. Corbitt meant you could go to Chihuahuita and communicate with the folks. That would help the *Herald* out quite a bit. Why, you could move up from office assistant to research . . . research specialist mighty fast. Your salary would go up, too, naturally."

"What *is* the salary, sir?" Alberto asked, but he was thinking about that title: research specialist. Sounded like a fancy name for a spy. Or a vendido. That's what his father would call him, a *pinche vendido*, selling out his people for half an acre of land.

". . . that's about standard for office boys," Corbitt was saying, "I mean office assistants, these days. Once you started doing research for us, we'd move it up from fifteen to eighteen a week."

Alberto took a deep breath and let it out through his nostrils, slowly, so that his indignation wouldn't show. "I'm afraid I can't be an office boy, Mr. Corbitt. I can't support my wife and two little girls on fifteen dollars a week. If you want, I can start being a research specialist right away. For twenty dollars a week. That's standard for high school graduates, isn't it?"

Alberto's eyes felt like lead. His father had once told him, *They can crush your heart, hijo, but don't let them break your huevos. That's the only advantage we have.*

Corbitt was looking at Gaines again. Finally, Corbitt said, "Call Peters in here, will you?"

Gaines stepped out of the office and yelled the name. A young fellow in a striped jacket limped into the room.

"What's up?" he said. He had a pencil tucked behind one ear, a cigarette behind the other.

"Peters," said Corbitt, "meet Albert Moralees. He's going to be your research specialist."

Alberto felt a pinch in his chest.

"My what?" said Peters, eyeing Alberto from hair to socks.

"He's going to be your link to Chihuahuita," said Gaines. "Your inside man."

"Chihuahuita ain't my beat, Chief," Peters said to the fat man.

"It is now, Peters," said Corbitt. "We're giving you a column. *Barrio News*. And Moralees here, he's going to get the news, and you're going to write it. Any complaints?"

"Hell no, Chief! A column? Hot tamales! Hey, Moralees, your name rhymes with tamales!"

"My name is Alberto Morales, Mr. Peters." The pinch had moved down to Alberto's groin.

"Show the man around, Peters," said Corbitt. "Then give him an assignment. Might as well break that column in *pronto*. When you bring your birth certificate in, Moralees, we'll get your contract ready."

"Congratulations, Moralees," Gaines said, slapping Alberto on the back.

Alberto did not thank the men. He followed Peters out of Corbitt's office, wringing his hat like a mop. Research specialist. Rosemary would like the sound of that.

"This here's *my* desk," said Peters. "My typewriter. My chair. My ashtray. You're gonna work on the street. Go get yourself a notebook from honey pie over there." He jerked his thumb in the direction of Miss Lind, who was filing her nails in the front office.

"I need a notebook," Alberto mumbled to her.

"No kidding?" she said, her file suspended.

"No kidding," Alberto said. She opened the bottom drawer of her desk, took a long, thin notebook from a pile, and handed it over to Alberto. On the cover, it said *Reporter's Notebook*.

"Go out and get me some news," Peters said behind him, the man's tobacco breath hanging on Alberto's neck. "But don't be giving me any opinions, Moralees. All I want from you is facts. Information. Keep your tamale-brained opinions to yourself. Flunkies don't give opinions, do they, Miss Lind?"

No señor, thought Alberto, gripping his hat in his fist. He was no ditchdigger. A ditchdigger would've already punched this cabrón's teeth out of his mouth. But he could hear Rosemary already. She would want to go down to the drugstore right away to telephone her father and give him the good news. *Albert got a real job, Daddy. He's training to be a reporter for the* El Paso Herald. *They even gave him a reporter's notebook.*

They're Just Silly Rabbits

I never knew Zulema's real name. I guess you could say that was a sign, if you believe in such things, which I didn't at the time. I knew that she was very different from me, that she was white, and had a legacy of gender oppression politics to stand behind her lesbianism, that she was privileged enough to pursue a degree in art history rather than in something practical like bilingual education counseling, that her family's roots in the country did not extend fourteen generations, that her grandmother had never picked corn or lived in a boxcar. Zulema *had* spent time on trains, though, traveling through India, China, Mexico, not as a tourist, she said, but as an artist tapping into the mysteries of the Third World. It was when she returned from Mexico that she legally changed her name and swore by the feet of her guru to join her life to a woman of color. At first, she would not acknowledge that I, as a Chicana, fit that description. But she liked it when I spoke Spanish, especially when we made love and I called her corazón.

I once said that Zulema had saved me because she'd pulled me, like a bullfighter's suit of lights, out of the closet. But Zulema hated that metaphor (although she refused to use the word hate). Anything that even intimated cruelty to animals distressed her, and my metaphor, colorful and folkloric as it was, she said, was about butchery, not beauty, and therefore not applicable to something as sacred as woman-love. I was not a poet, nor an artist, and there were nights when I'd escape to George's Bar and order a double cheeseburger, medium rare, with my Corona. We had our differences. Problem is, her differences seemed somehow more important than mine. Her morality, her politics, everything was spiritual, and I was afraid of her judgment and her scorn.

The end started with the rabbits. I never really understood

Zulema's obsession with protecting animals, but I think it had something to do with the theory of reincarnation, something about tending and respecting the soul, as well as the body, of all forms of life. Maybe Zulema's philosophy was just too esoteric for me; she believed herself a relative to rocks and flies.

"Do you think animals have ego?" she asked me one Sunday as we strolled through City Park. It was only the middle of September in Iowa City, but already the oaks and willows had started to turn, splashes of scarlet and gold in every direction.

"I think they have brains," I said, apprehensive already at what sounded like the beginning of another humanist versus animalist conversation, "and that they can probably think in some fundamental way. But I doubt they're developed enough mentally to have ego."

"So you think having an ego is progress?"

"It's evolution, at least."

"You really are so left brained, aren't you?"

"What's wrong with being logical?"

She shrugged and linked her arm in mine. "That's what I'm trying to find the answer to, you know, in my art."

Zulema was truly horrified by the incident of the rabbits. We had been invited to a brunch out in the country at the home of a couple of "politically correct" dykes—women who (as Zulema explained it to me before going), though they exercise no oppression over their sisters, be they First World, Third World, Differently-Abled, Bulimic, Anorexic, Overweight, Alcoholic, or whatever (as long, of course, as they belong to the Amazon Party), live according to the belief that the female sex does not need the male sex for anything. Naturally, Zulema did not agree. With all her spiritual preoccupation, she could not comprehend, much less condone, a politics that perpetuated what she called a "karmic imbalance," especially not after the Harmonic Convergence.

But the brunch was really very nice—in that way that white women have of being "nice" when they think that everyone agrees with them. The farmhouse had bay windows and polished, hardwood floors and smelled of freshly baked sourdough bread; the potluck became a buffet of homemade vegetarian and pasta dishes. Everyone ate hungrily. I noticed my green chile enchilada casserole, made with the last of the chile verde that my grandmother's sister sent us every

August from New Mexico, was the first dish to disappear. The only uncomfortable moment while we ate came when a cosmetologist seated beside Zulema on the futon started telling her that she had chosen cosmetology as her career solely to explode the myth of feminine beauty that had been imposed by the patriarchy. Zulema, in her sweetest voice, responded:

"Do you know that some of my best friends are men? Even my guru, whose feet I've kissed many times."

The den inside that farmhouse became an instant vacuum, and the silence that it bred was so thick, it cast a shadow. The shadow fell squarely over Zulema and me.

"That was good," I whispered. "Now we can watch them all turn into witches and tear our guts out with their fingernails."

She turned to look at me and said, louder than she needed to, "There sure is a lot of hot air in here."

I don't know whose idea it was to go out and see the rabbits, but soon there was a line of Amazons parading through the back door, carefully not glancing in our direction.

"I think it's time to go," I said, but the cosmetologist turned back and urged us to see the "bunnies" before we left.

Outside, the ideological differences between the dykes and ourselves seemed less oppressive. Maybe our politically correct brunchmates were interested in initiating us into their sisterhood and were disposed to tolerate our incorrectness. Maybe they just wanted to taunt us.

"See," said the cosmetologist, pointing to the rabbit warren. "Those are the boys over there and the girls over here."

"Sounds like she's trying to teach us a lesson," I mumbled into Zulema's ear. To the cosmetologist I said, "I guess they don't fuck like rabbits, as they say."

"There's usually a big barbecue after the mating season," said the cosmetologist. "You should come back for that. Nothing better than male rabbit on the spit."

"You only eat the male rabbits?" Zulema nearly screamed.

One of the hostesses grew red splotches in her face, but the other one said, "We don't really eat them. We just like seeing their balls roast."

Zulema and I left without saying good-bye. We walked through a fallow cornfield so that Zulema could scream her indignation. I had to hold her and stroke her hair to get her temper and pressure down.

Zulema had a delicate heart, and any kind of crisis would send meteors shooting through her veins. We sat on dry weeds until she got some color in her face, and then we walked back to town, hand in hand, past green and gold fields that would soon be harvested.

When we got home, Zulema locked herself in her studio and said she had an idea for a painting, a project that kept her away from school for a whole week. She never showed me her work before she finished it, and, as she hadn't completed this painting before she left me, I never got to see it. I don't know, now, if it was one of the pieces she took with her on her trip to New Mexico, or one of the pieces she burned. But, the incident of the rabbits shocked her so much that all the drawings and collages she made after that experience always bore a rabbit's foot in one corner. To tell you the truth, I thought she was overreacting. "They're just silly rabbits," I told her one night, never imagining how grave that stupid comment of mine would be.

The fall semester was ending at last. Zulema and I were making plans for our Christmas break. She wanted us to go to an ashram in Santa Cruz to learn how to commune with the ocean and to experience liberation from our egos. I wanted us to stay in Iowa City for once. I was attracted by the image of the empty town, buried in snow and silence. I had fantasies of long mornings in bed, drinking cappuccino, eating cinammon rolls, watching movies on the VCR. But as usual, Zulema was looking for something else. She was not interested in resting. "I want to learn. I want to travel," she told me. "I want to find the meaning of life."

I was not willing to spend what little energy I had left after a long semester trying to find "the meaning of life," especially not during vacation. For that we had Socrates and his compadres. Sometimes Zulema's obsessions felt like a last straw.

We decided that she would go to the ashram and talk to waves, and I would spend the holidays with my family in Chicago and then return to Iowa City to reconnect with my reading and catch up on all my correspondence. It had been three years since I'd written to my friends from the Colegio de México, and with all the new episodes that Zulema had produced in my life, I was sure that each of my letters would be an adventure. For my straight, chilanga friends, the story of my coming out would be a new kind of telenovela.

Our plans were made. Zulema managed to find a flight to San José at the last moment, and I flew with her (in a lowrider with wings that reeked of mothballs) to Chicago, where she would make her connection to the West Coast.

Everything changed in Chicago. When we stepped into the airport, we discovered that my brother had either forgotten to pick me up or was going to be late. Zulema's flight didn't leave for nearly two hours, so we would be able to have our Kahluas in private. Forty-five minutes later, my brother appeared in the bar, grumbling that he'd been looking for me all over the pinche airport. He took a seat and ordered a beer.

He had bad news, he said. Grandma had been diagnosed with cancer in the bone marrow, and the doctors had not given her more than half a year. Neither he nor my dad had wanted to say anything on the phone, to keep me from worrying. They'd also kept quiet to prevent me from disagreeing with their "new plans."

Grandma wanted to return to New Mexico, to die in the land of her gente. But, before raising her arms and surrendering to her destiny, she wanted to make a pilgrimage to the Sanctuary of Chimayó, a little chapel just north of Santa Fe. According to Grandma, there was a pit of miraculous dirt inside that chapel that healed any kind of illness. Her last wishes were to go to that place and rub her body with that dirt, and, since I was on vacation, and since I always got stuck with ridiculous missions, I had been chosen to escort Grandma on her pilgrimage.

I didn't go for the idea. Grandma's imminent death was shock enough; I did not need to be electrocuted with the "new plans." I suddenly saw visions of a chapel in the graveyard surrounded by blind, lame, and diseased people—all digging desperately in the pit of miraculous dirt.

"No way!" I told my brother. "First of all, Armando, you know I'm afraid of flying. If Grandma wants to return to Santa Fe or go to this Chimayó place, o lo que sea, you or my 'apá can take her. I'm not going. Why didn't you tell me beforehand? Forget it! I'm not going!"

Zulema, who had listened to the conversation like a kid in the presence of a miracle, stared at me and shook her head. Suddenly, she covered her face with her hands and started to cry.

Armando and I looked at each other without understanding anything. Then Zulema seemed to change her mind about something, and abruptly she stood up, spilling my brother's beer on the table. She grabbed her bag and portfolio and hurried out of the bar, her face all smeared and her nose still running. I ran after her, of course, but she didn't want to talk to me.

"What's wrong with you?" I said. "Where are you going?" I tried to come close, but she stepped back.

"I don't want you to touch me, please," she said, adding that, although she didn't owe me any explanations, out of respect for the three years of our relationship, she was going to tell me what had clicked in her mind when she heard my reaction to my grandmother's request. I don't remember Zulema's exact words. That day remains the most embarrassing one in my life, and my memory has managed to embalm it in cobwebs; but the following is a pretty faithful reconstruction of what Zulema told me the day she marched out of my life.

"I remembered your comment about the rabbits, remember? That seemed like such a heartless thing to say, and it showed such a lack of respect for life itself, that I couldn't even respond to it. You don't know how many nights I cried because of what your comment told me about you. But my love for you was greater than my love for the rabbits, and I let it pass, thinking you would change. That maybe I could help you come to appreciate the things of the soul.

"But I see that you can't do that, yet. Perhaps your spirit is too young and needs to live more lifetimes to sensitize itself. Or perhaps it was very damaging for you to grow up in the Midwest, so far away from your land and your people, and maybe you really aren't responsible for your lack of understanding. I don't know what it is, but when I saw your reaction just now, when I realized that you just can't comprehend the importance that journey has for your grandmother, the faith she has in that sacred earth, I became conscious of the one thing that has always separated us. I don't blame you for not understanding her, but I do know that I can't stay with you any longer. You're the one who speaks the language, but I'm the one who understands the word corazón.

"Now I know what I've been missing and what I have to do. I *need* to go to that chapel. I'm going back to Iowa City right now for some paintings I want to take, and I'm going to cancel my trip to Santa Cruz. Tell your grandmother not to worry. Tell her I want to make that pilgrimage with her and heal myself with that earth. Tell her it would make me very happy to go with her. I can't do anything to save the lives of those poor rabbits, but, maybe in this case, I *can* help."

With Zulema, it was not possible to argue or to beg. But I did both in a matter of minutes. I started out by yelling that she was an arrogant, egocentric, pseudo-hippie artist trying to appropriate both my grandmother and my culture, and from there, I humiliated myself even more. I followed her all over the airport while she bought a ticket for the next flight back to Iowa and then investigated the flights to New Mexico. She didn't pay any attention to me; not when I insulted her or when I implored her to please not leave like this without at least giving me a chance to fix what I had done (although the truth is, I didn't *know* what I had done; I only knew that a part of my life was about to turn to dust).

"This hurts me more than you will ever know. I hope you can find another place while I'm gone. Tell your grandmother there's a flight to Albuquerque at 5:45 Friday afternoon. If she wants to go with me, she can meet me right here at 4:30. I've reserved a first class seat for her."

"She can't pay first class, and I don't think she'll go with you, Zulema. What makes you think you can take my place?"

"I'm not taking your place. Just tell her I'm going to make the pilgrimage myself."

"Why are you doing this, Zulema? You don't know anything about this pilgrimage or this place, but you're going anyway, another mystery for you to tap into. You're *so* sensitive and spiritually evolved, you'll believe anything."

"Do you see that we're at a crossroads?" she said. "This was meant to happen."

Those were the last words Zulema spoke to me. With that, and with the sidelong look she gave me, I knew everything was lost. She did not respect me anymore. We had agreed that the moment one of us lost respect for the other and couldn't look at her openly, we would have to separate. The moment came and was gone like any other tornado in the heartland.

Zulema passed through the same door we had entered on our arrival from Cedar Rapids, went down the stairs, and strode to the commuter plane. The Chicago wind disheveled the hair that I had stroked for three years. I remembered the blonde roots pushing up into the dark brown that Zulema thought would match her name. Something about that image made me weep. My breath fogged the cold glass. Tears blurred the lights of the runway.

My brother was still waiting for me in the bar, watching a Bears game and working on his second beer when I sat down beside him.

"What's your *problem*?" he asked, scowling, "and where the hell is Zulema? 'Apá's gonna be all worried. Are we leaving yet, or what? We still have to get your luggage."

"Armando, please don't say anything about this to Dad," I said, wiping my face with a bar napkin. "Weird things are happening that neither you nor I can understand. Do you think Grandma wants to go with Zulema to Chimayó?"

"With Zulema? Are you crazy?"

"I can't take her, Armando."

"Grandma likes Zulema and everything, but she doesn't like what you two are doing. Anyway, this Chimayó thing is private. It's a family thing."

"Well, I hope she says yes, because Zulema isn't going to California anymore. She's booked a flight to Albuquerque on Friday afternoon; Grandma can go first class. Zulema says she wants to heal herself with this miraculous dirt, too."

"You two are safadas, man," said Armando. "Why Zulema and not you? You're the granddaughter. She's not even Mexican."

"Zulema's more spiritual than I am. I don't *believe* that Chimayó stuff, Armando." I told him about the rabbit incident.

"Zulema doesn't see a difference between rabbits getting killed and Grandma dying? You call that spirituality? She's just being nosy, como siempre. Anyway, Grandma doesn't need to go first class; she just needs to go."

"She'll be more comfortable in first class, Armando. It's a long way to New Mexico."

"How would you know?"

"Look, Armando, get off my case. I've had enough lessons for today. I don't see *you* doing anything to help Grandma; don't talk about me. I'm not the only one who has a responsibility here."

"You're always letting Zulema tell you what to do." He shook his head. "Ella no sabe nada."

"Zulema's gone," I said, only then realizing that she had left me, or maybe, that we had never been together. I thought of Grandma, of losing Grandma, and knew there was no way I'd let her go without a fight. To Zulema, Chimayó would be an image for a painting; to Grandma, it was a place of healing and history. It was a place where faith was created, not through workshops or seminars, but through struggle and negotiation.

"Let's go, Armando," I said. I wanted to get home and call Zulema, leave a message on her machine, tell her Grandma didn't need a tour guide, after all.

La Mariscal

As usual, The Red Canary was still empty at ten o'clock. Mexicans didn't start their whoring till after midnight, and Jack Dublin knew it would be the perfect place to sit and drink quietly for a few hours, maybe even buy himself some company for the rest of the evening, once the tequila seeped into his veins.

His colleagues from the Sociology Department were watching the strip show across the street at the Mona Lisa Club, the most popular brothel on the Mariscal. Jack had wanted to be alone, a habit he'd gotten into even before leaving Boston. The only other Bostonian habit he still cultivated was patronizing the Combat Zone, called La Mariscal here on the border.

Jack had been hoping for something to pull him out of Boston and help him forget the memories of his ex-wife. Then, with the luck of the Irish, one of his grad school buddies, now a tenured professor at a university that fancied itself Harvard-on-the-Border, had invited Jack to fly out and do a conference and come prepared for being offered a position in the Sociology Department. After three and a half years of living on the border, Jack considered himself a native.

The Red Canary was sponsoring a Tex-Mex band, and Jack knew that the place would be swarming with obreros later, their clothes and hands still caked with mud or paint or grease or whatever else they worked with. Jack let his eyes adjust to the scarlet glow of the lightbulbs and noticed that the big cage over the bar was empty. Jack slid into a booth far from the stage, wondering what had happened to the bird, the mascot of The Red Canary, which was really a white cockatoo with a red crest.

The tall, monkey-faced girl with the hairy calves was waitressing tonight. He ordered his usual shot of Herradura tequila with a Cruz

Blanca draft as a chaser and asked the monkey-faced girl if the bird had escaped.

"Ese pinche pájaro," she said, waving her hand at the cage. "He got a job on the other side by now, making more dollars than all of us."

Jack laughed, understanding her allusion to migrant workers across the border. But maybe she didn't mean that at all. He was always reading sociological implications into people's statements. No matter how drunk he got, Jack was always a sociologist. He stretched his legs out in the booth and rubbed his palms together. He felt ripe tonight, eager to yield to the great cactus spirit. He ran his eyes over the bar and nodded to Gregorio, the bartender. The only customers sitting at the bar were a GI in uniform and his girlfriend.

The monkey-faced girl brought his drinks and stroked his hand with her fingers as she gave him the napkin full of limes.

"Me llamo Magda," she reminded him and walked away. Jack watched her move between the tables, her leather miniskirt and flouncy, low-cut blouse speaking of her flexibility: a leather woman or a girl in ruffles. Jack knocked back the Herradura and squeezed a lime wedge between his teeth. He looked towards the bar again, where the GI had fallen off his stool, and realized that the girl beside the GI was a working girl, though she didn't look it from the way she was dressed. It was really the drunken soldier who gave her away. With her smooth, olive complexion, the bloom of peacock feathers in her blue-black hair, her embroidered Mexican dress, she looked more like an Aztec princess. Maybe she wasn't a working girl, after all. The GI got back on his stool and looped his arm around her neck. Wrong, Jack, he said to himself, taking a long draw on his beer.

The band broke the silence of the bar with a polka, and Gregorio, the bartender, hooted in approval. Jack sat back to listen. The band's name was lettered on the face of the bass: LOS GUAJOLOTES DEL CHAMIZAL. The Chamizal Turkeys. (The bird motif was popular in this bar.) Apart from the bass player, the other Turkeys were a guitarist and a man on a push-button accordion, the three of them in sombreros and scuffed boots, singing about contraband.

Jack glanced over at the bar again. The soldier was trying to get the Aztec princess to dance, but she kept shaking her head, and Gregorio came over and said something to the soldier. The GI plopped himself on the stool and chugged his beer like a petulant boy. Jack called the monkey-faced girl over to order himself another Herradura and to send the Aztec princess a drink on him. When she brought Jack's second tequila, the monkey-faced girl wasn't as friendly as she'd been the last time. Jack tipped her five dollars, twice as much as he'd paid for the drinks.

The Aztec princess turned around on the stool to face him. She held the snifter that Gregorio had just set before her between her two middle fingers and dipped her head gently in a gesture of thanks. Jack raised his shot glass, toasting with her at a distance. She kept her eyes on him as she sipped the amber liquid in the snifter, then lowered her eyelids and turned to face the GI beside her, his head lolling over the bar.

Jack polished off his tequila, sucked on another lime, and knew he was in danger. That's all he needed was to become infatuated with one of these girls. He took his wallet out and removed a folded piece of paper that he always carried, the last letter to his ex-wife that he'd never finished and never sent, and that he carried as an amulet against dangerous situations like this one. He unfolded the paper and read his words:

Dear Barbara,

I'm sitting here on the pier of George's Island listening to the tolling of buoys, thinking about hatred, trying to decide when it was that I first started to hate you. The gulls come in swirls, circling above the buoys and the flat, gray Atlantic, screaming to the nothingness of the old fort on the island. The birds are a good analogy for our marriage. Migrating between hope and despair while circling above us were the vultures of your lesbian friends, feeding you the carrion of our relationship, screeching their triumph at the one who had walled himself up in his fort of nothingness on his island of self-pity.

There is not much to write about, actually, and the sun bores hot holes in my back as I sit here hunched over this notebook, trying to decide when my hatred for you started, a cold, gray wave that smashes any trace of nostalgia. Behind me, men and women spread their picnics on the grass, fly kites together, pose for pictures in their bright smiles and dark glasses. How many of those women, I wonder, will turn into vultures like you did? How many marriages will be pecked to death by those of your kind?

Jack read the letter twice, forcing himself to remember all those nights he'd waited up for Barbara, only to have her sneak in just before sunrise, smelling of tobacco and a perfume she didn't own. It had taken him a long time to figure out what she was doing and then even more time to believe it, and all the while his balls were shrinking, and his hair was going gray.

Jack folded the letter again and replaced it in his wallet, feeling braver now, and like he wanted to take the monkey-faced girl to one of the back rooms of The Red Canary. But the Aztec princess was looking at him again, and the GI had fallen asleep on the bar. Jack picked up his beer and ambled over to the Aztec princess.

"Is he with you?" he asked her, standing behind the drunken soldier. She shook her head, and Jack had Gregorio come around to help him get the GI to his feet and out the door.

"Go home, now, amigo," Jack said to the soldier as they stood out on the sidewalk. "Sleep it off at home, buddy." When he came back inside, the Aztec princess was sitting with her hands folded in her lap, her back straight as a flagpole as she listened to another polka from the Guajolotes.

"Can I buy you another drink?" he asked her and waited for her to accede before he straddled the stool beside her. "Gregorio!" he called, "another round, por favor!" And then, to the princess he said, "My name is Jack. What's yours?"

She had brought all of her hair over one shoulder, a blue-black cascade into which she turned her face when she spoke. "Susana," she said, "pleased to meet you." In spite of her accent, her voice was mellifluous.

Gregorio brought their drinks, and Jack laid a twenty on the bar, telling the bartender to keep supplying them till the money ran out. Then he gave Gregorio a five for himself.

"You're very beautiful, Susana," Jack told her after they'd toasted to each other's health. "I don't think I've ever seen you in this place."

When she shook her head, her eyelids trembled. She wore no makeup and smelled of honeysuckle. "I'm just waiting for my sister," she said.

"I understand," Jack said, touching the small bone at her wrist. She had a dimple when she smiled. "Do you like the music?" he asked. He stroked her forearm.

"Look, señor," she said, pulling her arm away, "I'm from Chihuahua, and I'm just waiting for my sister." She paused, took a sip of brandy, and added: "I don't work here."

"I understand," Jack said again. He was beginning to feel a little breathless. The Herradura was doing its job. The Aztec princess was doing hers.

Los Guajolotes del Chamizal had filled the place sooner than he'd expected, and Jack was glad he'd come up to the bar where he could watch the dancing from a distance. He got an idea. If Susana wanted to play the coy mistress, Jack could play Don Juan.

"Excuse me," he told her and went up to the monkey-faced girl to ask her to dance, slipping another five in her cleavage before she could say no.

When he came back to his stool, Susana would not look at him.

"Magda says she isn't your sister," he whispered in her ear.

"I did not say she was," said Susana. "My sister is the nurse in the back."

"Oh," said Jack, raising Susana's hand to his lips and kissing each of the tiny pyramids of her knuckles. "Forgive me, Susana," he said, "but you do strange things to me. Your beauty is dangerous." He blushed at the triteness of his words and threw back another tequila. His beer was getting warm.

"What do you mean 'strange things'?" she asked. "Do you like to do strange things?"

"You speak English very well, Susana," Jack said. He himself hadn't noticed the double entendre. "You're very intelligent," he added. He touched the peacock feathers in her hair. It was everything he could do to not press her against him. For a very long time, Jack had not felt more than lust for a woman, more than the primal urge to feel her naked and vulnerable beneath him. Tonight, he wanted to serve Susana, kneel before her and taste her native blood, swallow the Aztec seed of her, save her from the cage of The Red Canary. The pale Catholic girls of the Combat Zone, even the China girls, for all their willingness and experience, did not hold a candle up to this Aztec princess. He felt her hand on his thigh and nearly burst his pants.

"Excuse me," she said to him, climbing off the stool, "just a moment." He watched her squeeze through the crowd as she made her way to where the monkey-faced girl was wiping ashtrays. When Susana returned, she had a pack of Raleighs with her.

"I didn't know you smoked," Jack said, disappointed.

"Does it molest you?"

What a perfect way of putting it, Jack thought, although he knew she had just mistranslated "bother." Yes, it bothered him. He hated the taste of tobacco in a woman's mouth. He couldn't lie to her. He had to let her know that she was special, and special ladies didn't smoke, in his book. As soon as Barbara had started smoking, Jack had known he was losing her.

"I don't mind the smoke," he said to Susana, ignoring the matchbook she'd placed in front of him for him to light her cigarette. "It's the image that *molests* me. I don't like to see a woman with a cigarette in her mouth, much less an Aztec princess like you."

"I will go to the bathroom," she said in a severe voice that didn't match her coyness. She took the pack of Raleighs and her drink and stalked off toward the back of the bar, where the rooms were. One of her high heels caught on the rug, and she stumbled. Jack had to smile. His Aztec princess had a temper. He called Gregorio and asked if Susana worked in The Red Canary. He wanted to double-check.

"Her name is Berta," said Gregorio, "but she uses Susana with the gringos." Gregorio winked and poured Jack another Herradura. The Turkeys took a break.

"Save our places, Gregorio," Jack said. "This won't take long." He swallowed the tequila.

At the entrance to the hallway in the back, a fat woman in a nurse's uniform whom he'd never seen before had Jack unzip his pants to show her he was clean. Jack caught some of his pubic hair in the zipper.

"Fondo a la derecha," the nurse told him where to go, holding a white can with a red cross painted on it in front of Jack. He folded up a dollar bill, pushed it through the slit, then walked down the corridor to find Susana.

She was still dressed, sitting on the edge of the bed finishing her cigarette. Behind her in a black velvet painting on the wall, a voluptuous Indian maiden offered her bronze breasts to an armored conquistador. Jack saw that his Aztec princess had applied lipstick and false eyelashes. The room reeked of tobacco. She got up to close the door and rinsed her mouth out with brandy. Jack tried to kiss her, but she turned her head.

"I don't kiss for money," she said.

Los derechos de La Malinche

Dicen que no tengo duelo, Llorona
Porque no me ven llorar.
Hay muertos que no hacen ruido, Llorona
Y es más grande su penar.
—"La Llorona"

No me voy a disculpar. Después de tantos años, hasta nuestra lengua ha cambiado. Es posible que ni me entiendas. Es posible que mis palabras todavía estén coaguladas. Pero no puedo flaquear. Nunca es tarde cuando la dicha es buena. He venido a traerte tunas. Míralas. Qué frescas. Qué rojas. Su jugo se desliza sobre las letras de tu nombre. Le hacía falta este toque de sangre a tu lápida. Ahora tu apodo —EL PAPACITO— se puede apreciar mejor.

Papá, anoche te volví a soñar. En la película del sueño, estaba toda la familia en una fiesta, una quinceañera o un bautismo, alguna iniciación. Tú estabas sentado en una mesa, vestido de etiqueta, tu camisa de seda blanca, tu corbata de moño. Tenías más de 52 años. Parecías abuelo con canas y dos largos surcos a cada lado de la frente donde tu cuero cabelludo lucía como cera. Parecía que dormías.

A tu lado, en una mesa aparte, mi hermano te escudriñaba. Agachaba la cabeza y te miraba con terror y tristeza. Yo me acerqué a tu mesa. En cuclillas y con la quijada en el mantel, te observé igual que mi hermano. De repente se te movió la cara. Una mueca de dolor, un jalón de labios y ojos que me hizo brincar y gritarle a mi hermano.

"Sí ", me dijo mi hermano. "Ya lo vi".

Volteé y te miré de nuevo, y de nuevo se movió tu cuerpo. Te estirabas como un gato después de una larga siesta. Me eché a correr, a decirle a todos que estabas vivo, que te estabas moviendo, pero nadie me hacía caso.

Regresé a tu mesa. En un sillón, directamente en frente de ti, mi hermana le daba el pecho a su recién nacida. Tus ojos se abrieron como grietas. Miraste un tiempo a mi hermana, luego dijiste:

"Hija, tráeme de comer".

Mi hermana te ignoró como si no te hubiese oído. Sentí un dolor muy grande al saber que tenías hambre, tú que nunca comías, que le hacías "Fo!" a los platillos humeantes que te preparaba mi abuela para que dejaras de tomar.

Al ver que mi hermana no te respondía, te pusiste de pie y pediste comida otra vez, pero en cuanto diste el primer paso, tus piernas se doblaron y fuiste a dar al suelo. Te levantaste y te caíste dos veces más. Para la segunda caída, tu cuerpo ya estaba descompuesto. La ropa se te había podrido y tu piel parecía carne cruda, agusanada. Las piernas se te habían volteado y ya no tenías labios, sólo esa dentadura blanca y postiza.

Pasó un tiempo en el sueño, pero después regresamos a ese lugar, que se había transformado en avión con asientos azules. Tú estabas sentado al fondo del avión, y me acuerdo que se te oía claramente decir que tenías mucha hambre, pero nadie, nadie más que yo, te escuchaba. Me fui para atrás y te dije:

"Pero estás muerto".

"Sí ", dijiste, "la parte mala está muerta, pero la parte buena sigue viva y tiene hambre".

Recorrí el avión, gritándole a mis tíos y tías lo que me habías dicho, pero era como hablar con muertos.

Decidí darte de comer. Te llevé un cartón de leche y unas galletitas de mantequilla envueltas en papel parafinado. Te serví un vaso grande de leche bien cremosa. Me pediste que te acompañara. Pensé que la leche se me iba a cortar en la panza con todo el mezcal que había tomado la noche anterior, pero me serví un vaso de todas maneras. Al pelarle el papel a una de las galletas, me di cuenta que era una hostia.

De pronto me dieron ganas de acariciarte. Te me hacías muy inocente allí sentado con tu leche y tus galletas, como un niño jugando a la primera comunión. Cerré los ojos y acaricié tu cara, pegando mi cachete con el tuyo, pero cuando abrí los ojos, estaba acariciando al cartón de leche.

Después escuché tu voz. Me dijiste que le pidiera a todos en el avión que escribieran algo de ti o algo de esta situación. Fui y les di lápiz y papel a todos, y pedí que cumplieran con tus deseos, pero nadie quería escribir. Decían que pronto llegaríamos a nuestro destino y que no iban a tener tiempo de escribir nada. Los insulté a todos. Ya no podía más con esa frialdad.

"Siempre lo han tratado igual", les grité. "Y todavía tienen la desfachatez de criticarme por no haber ido a su funeral. Váyanse todos al demonio. Yo voy a escribir. No me importa llegar o no llegar a donde vamos. No me bajo de aquí hasta que termine mi carta".

La cámara se enfocó en el papel y claramente se distinguían las palabras que escribía, mi letra la de una niña de nueve años que apenas empieza a tener confianza con la cursiva. Lo más raro es que te escribí en inglés:

> Dear Dad,
> If you want to heal your body, you have to rest a lot and you should hold this crystal pyramid in your right hand so that its energy can go up your arm and heal your body.

Dad, tú a mí me escribiste dos veces. La primera fue una carta para cuando cumplí seis años. Me decías que no me cortara el pelo. Que obedeciera a mi abuela. Que el cheque de un dólar que acompañaba la carta era para dulces y chocolates. Pasaron veintiún años antes de recibir la postal que me mandaste desde Las Vegas. Me prometiste que ya que sabías mi dirección, ibas a escribir más seguido. Nunca más volví a leer tu letra.

Decía mi abuela que estabas muy amargado por lo que yo había elegido, "Esa vida anormal, esa vida sin hombre". Antes, la culpable de tu cirrosis era mi madre por haberte dejado. Después eran mis hermanos y tus hermanos por tratarte como un cero a la izquierda. Luego me cayó el muerto a mí. De ti, papi, la culpa se desprendía como el polen.

En vez de venir a tu entierro, me escapé a México, pero aún allá me alcanzaba el polvo frío de tu aliento.

En Teotihuacán, por la Avenida de los Muertos, una india vendía amuletos de cristal en forma de pirámide. Uno en particular me habló. Era el Templo del Sol en miniatura, sus cuatro caras reflejando la luz verde de la tarde. Lo tomé en la mano derecha y sentí que un arco iris me entraba por el brazo. Sabía que este amuleto me iba a proteger de ti.

Después en Guanajuato, en un museo de muertos momificados

por las mismas piedras del panteón, cuerpos con lenguas y vellos, tendidos en cajas de vidrio esperando el beso del amor, le acaricié los dedos de los pies a una momia china. No lo hice por ti. No fue ninguna manifestación de honor a tu muerte.

Entiéndeme. No vine al funeral porque no te quería ver dentro de una caja, rodeado de flores y lágrimas artificiales como cualquier rey del cine. Dicen que te veías muy guapo, papacito como siempre. Que traías un traje blanco y que el ataúd era de madera muy fina. Me contó mi madre que un compadre tuyo te llevó un ramo de gardenias. "Era una costumbre de mi compadre", contó el compadre, "en las noches de farra, comprarle un ramito de gardenias a una viejita que siempre estaba en la esquina de la Lerdo y el Malecón".

En Oaxaca, una noche de mucho mezcal, sentadas mi mujer y yo a la orilla de la plaza principal, rodeadas de niños vendiendo chiclets y flores, canastas y boleadas, escuché la canción de "La Llorona" dos veces, y le compré un ramo de gardenias a la vendedora más pequeña del mundo. Esa noche viniste a visitarme, así como siempre antes me visitabas en cada una de mis borracheras. Te eché en seguida. Abrí la boca sobre el excusado y te dejé salir, algo amargo y espeso que se pegaba a la taza como el atole de la muerte. No me di cuenta hasta al otro día que fueron las gardenias las que te habían traído. Por eso, nunca más he comprado gardenias.

No me voy a disculpar. Cuando me avisaron de tu embolia, sentí una gran calma. El coágulo de palabras en mi garganta al fin se empezó a deslizar, y al fin pude soltar la sangre de tu recuerdo. Por eso he venido a traerte tunas, la fruta sagrada de Huitzilopochtli.

Cuando llegó el hombre blanco y barbudo a la celda de la Malinche, ella estaba rezándole a Coatlicue, diosa de la muerte. Venía con el barbudo otro hombre vestido todo de negro con un cuello blanco. El hombre era de su raza, la misma cara de bronce, manos de esclavo, ojos de vendido.

"¿Qué quieres?" le dijo Malintzín al vendido.

El hablaba dos idiomas, igual que ella, y tenían uno en común.

"Este señor quiere saber si tú eres la intérprete".

Ella miro al barbudo. Tenía pelos hasta en el pecho y sus piernas parecían de gallina. En la ingle le colgaba el símbolo del nuevo dios.

No titubeó. "Sí, soy la intérprete. Pero estoy ocupada".

El vendido tradujo su respuesta. El barbudo echó la cabeza para atrás y le salió una carcajada de la boca. Su lengua parecía culebra enroscada entre los dientes. Cuando la miro de nuevo, había chispas de sangre en sus ojos. Le estiró la mano y dijo algo que el vendido no se ocupó de traducir.

"Estoy ocupada", repitió Malintzín, "estoy rezando".

Al oír el tono de su voz, el barbudo retiró la mano. Hubo un intercambio de palabras entre ellos y después el vendido le dijo:

"Este señor quiere saber dónde están tu rosario y tu cruz. Dice que no se puede rezar sin esas cosas. Dice que estás pecando, que él te viene a salvar".

Malintzín se empezó a marear. Le venía un ataque de palabras raras, palabras que no conocía, palabras secretas de las diosas. No quería que el extranjero escuchara su canto. Ese sí que era un pecado. Se le convulsionó el estómago y echó un líquido amargo a los pies del barbudo. Ya le venían las primeras sílabas. Tenía que escapar. Tenía que salir corriendo. Esas palabras no podían ser escuchadas por ningún hombre, blanco o de raza. Vomitó otra vez y le salió un camaleón. El barbudo brincó para atrás, gritando en su lengua extraña al vendido. El camaleón crecía y crecía, y de su boca salía un cascabel que repiqueteaba en las narices del barbudo.

"¡En el nombre del Padre, y del Hijo, y del Espíritu Santo!" intonaba el vendido, echándole a Malintzín gotas de ácido de un frasco que traía en la mano.

Poco a poco el mareo se le fue quitando. El esfuerzo la había agotado, pero al menos había logrado salvar a las palabras. Apenas podía respirar. Su cuerpo temblaba y el sudor que le escurría de los pelos de las axilas le quemaba como el ácido del vendido.

Sintió algo fresco contra los labios. El barbudo le había traído el jarrón de agua. Lo miró por unos momentos antes de beber. Luego, con manos de papel, con la ayuda del barbudo, alzó el jarrón y dejó que el agua del manantial la lavara por dentro y por fuera. El barbudo parecía entender lo que ella quería porque le subió el jarrón para que el agua le corriera por el pelo y la frente. Le dijo algo al vendido y el vendido tradujo:

"Dice que ya estás bautizada. Que viene mañana para llevarte a la misa matinal".

La Malinche no dijo nada. Sólo movió la cabeza de arriba abajo. En sus sienes escuchaba un concierto de cascabeles.

Esa noche, Marina se preparó bien. Con la ayuda de Coatlicue y Tonantzín, se irritó las paredes de su sexo con el pellejo espinoso de unas tunas, dejando que el jugo rojo de la fruta le chorreara las piernas. Después, se adornó el cabello con plumas de pavo real y se acostó en su petate. El barbudo llegó con el primer canto del gallo. Al darse cuenta que la mujer sangraba, sintió hervir la leche y apenas tuvo tiempo de bajarse el pañal. Cuando él se encontró en aquella hinchazón, en aquel nido de espinas donde su miembro se había atrapado como una culebra, sus gritos le salieron a borbotones. Nunca se había sentido Doña Marina tan dueña de su destino.

¿Te acuerdas, Papá, la vez que llegaste a la madrugada y quisiste forzar a mi mamá? Yo tenía tres años. Dormía en un catre en la recámara de ustedes. Me asusté cuando le escupiste esa palabra: ¡Cabrona! Y después viniste a taparme. Qué tal la vez que te vi orinando por la ventana del baño. Tú sabías que yo estaba allí. Hasta hiciste que te bailara el pirulí. Te confieso. Una noche en casa de mi abuela te escuché jadeando, el mismo ruido que hacía mi novio cuando yo lo masturbaba en el carro.

Cuando el barbudo le picó las faldas a la Malinche, ella ya sabía qué esperar. Su padre, el jefe de los tabasqueños, se lo había explicado todo un día antes de que vinieran los recaudadores de Moctezuma por ella. Lo que pasó con el barbudo no fue más que otro tributo a otro conquistador. Uno lampiño y hereje, y el otro no.

Mi abuela siempre me acusó de hereje. Decía que me iba a cocer en el infierno porque nunca rezaba el rosario y porque me comía la hostia sin haberme confesado. Lo que ella ignoraba es que tú, padre nuestro que estás en el cielo, me llevabas al matinée los sábados a la tarde y me alzabas la falda y me dabas el pan de cada día.

A diferencia de ti, mi novio era gringo y tenía barba, pero a él también le gustaba el cine. Lo que pasó con ese barbudo no fue más que otro tributo a otro conquistador.

Ahora, ya se acabaron las pleitesías. Estas tunas son los derechos que me violaste, las palabras secretas que me tragué.

Tengo el tuétano empapado. Acaba de caer uno de esos chaparrones que inunda hasta el desierto. La sangre del nopal que pintaba tu nombre se ha lavado con el agua. Tu piedra ha quedado limpia, EL PAPACITO fresco como el pasto del cementerio. Los cascabeles que escucho son mis propios dientes.

The Piñata Dream

I

What is your earliest remembered dream and your earliest memory, and what do you think they say about who you are today? Please write a paragraph for each part of the question.

"I've never thought about my earliest remembered dream. ~~I think this is like asking— I believe this may not be the first thing~~

"Shit!" She crumpled the paper and turned up the volume on her Walkman, keeping time with her pencil. The Alan Parsons Project was singing about confusion, a feeling swirling around in her own blood at this moment. She had come to the cemetery, one of her favorite places in Iowa City, to write the essay on the questionnaire, believing that the quiet graveyard in the hazy autumn morning would be just the place for her to remember her earliest dream.

Instead, she found herself thinking about her poetry class, about the poems they had workshopped so far that she could never have written. It wasn't because she didn't understand the assignments, or because she didn't know anything about life, as the professor had insinuated, but because she was a fiction writer, a storyteller, and she wrote story-poems. Hadn't they ever heard of narrative poetry and prose poetry? Oh, but the class didn't go for that. The professor was hung up on enjambment and didn't believe in prepositions. Even imagery was something less than allegory. Imagery, they said, was just concrete objects in words. A wheelbarrow didn't have to be symbolic of the womb of life and the story of creation. It was just a wheelbarrow, they insisted, a thing to carry dirt in and to catch the rain, as if the dirt and the rain weren't characters in the same plot.

The class was starting to constipate her, in every sense. And when anybody reminded her that she was the only 17-year-old ever to get a scholarship to the Iowa Writers' Workshop, she'd put her finger down her throat and gag as a response. She was also the only one in the Workshop who had a book of stories published. Besides, she was female and had a Mexican last name. Even though there was a town full of Mexicans fourteen miles away from Iowa City, even though there was a Chicano House on campus, Mexican Americans weren't exactly a constituency in the writers' community.

She opened her thermos, poured herself the dregs of her chamomile tea, and smoothed out the crumpled paper. Why couldn't she write this essay? She finally had the chance to string sentences together, but her memory was acting weird, shy almost. Right now, the only dream she remembered was the piñata dream, and only because it came as regularly as her period. She looked up at the nine-foot Black Angel that graced the tomb on which she always leaned and waited for the Angel's eyes to show and to slide down from her black forehead as they always did when she was underneath.

"I'll make a deal with you, Rodina," she said out loud when the Angel's eyes appeared. "If you help me remember, I'll come visit you every day, even in winter. If I don't write this essay, I can't go to the appointment. What do you say, Rodina?"

She had named the Angel after the woman whose tomb the giant statue guarded: Rodina Feldevertova. Another immigrant to the Midwest, just like X. Mary Espinosa. But Rodina's eyes rolled back into her head, and Mary knew that her only alternative now was to fake it. She took the clipping from *The Daily Iowan* out of her pocket and read it again to get her imagination pumping.

PANDORA'S JUNGLE

Where your dreams meet the Tarot

Hazel Eaves, L.I.C.S.W.

The alternative to counseling. For Womyn only. Learn how to release your own ills and blessings. Call for appointment or information. 362-7155.

Mary had called on Saturday, had gone over to meet this Hazel

Eaves and to get the questionnaire that she had to fill out before their first session. The last thing on the questionnaire was this essay that she couldn't write and that Hazel Eaves had told her was imperative as the foundation for the reading.

She looked out over the graveyard and felt lost. Sure, she could write a weird dream, a bizarre scene for a memory, but if the interpretation of the piñata dream depended on this essay, and this essay was only fiction, the interpretation wasn't going to work, and Mary would never know why the piñata dream had been haunting her for so long. How could she fake something as important as this? In her ears, Chuck Mangione was doing "Feels So Good." She took the headphones off, screwed the plastic cup back onto the thermos, and stuffed the Walkman and the thermos into her backpack. She touched the hem of the Black Angel's dress before leaving the tomb, then walked her bike to the asphalt path that led out of the cemetery. Hazel Eaves would just have to understand that after a month and a half of reading poetry and trying to exorcise the prose out of her poems, Mary couldn't write an essay. They'd just have to do something else for a foundation.

II

"Am I late? Your roommate said you were back here."

The husky voice startled Hazel out of her meditation. She sat up on her mat and looped the wires of her glasses behind her ears. The girl was wearing bright yellow bicycling tights, purple high-tops, and a black baseball cap with a red pitchfork as a logo.

"Not really," Hazel said. "I was planning to sit out here anyway. This'll be the last of Indian summer, I'm afraid." She reached an arm out to the girl. "Help an old lady up," she said, and the girl held her elbow out for support. "Let's go to the picnic table. Are you ready to explore Pandora's Jungle?"

"That's my unconscious, right?" said the girl.

"Right," said Hazel. "I like your cap. What's the pitchfork about?"

"El Paso Diablos," the girl answered as she slipped onto the bench across the table from Hazel. "The dust-devils of Dudley Field."

"A piece of home," said Hazel. "Why were you late? Having second thoughts?"

The girl ran her fingers over the carved teakwood box that held

Hazel's materials for the session. Hazel noticed that her nails were even closer to extinction than they had been on Saturday.

"I was in the cemetery trying to write that essay," the girl said, "but I didn't get very far."

"Let me see," said Hazel.

The girl unzipped her pack and pulled out the questionnaire. Hazel glanced down at the first page. Sagittarius. Only child. Catholic. First time away from home. "Why were you in the cemetery?" Hazel asked, flipping to the back of the questionnaire.

"I go there sometimes," the girl said.

"I don't see the essay."

The girl took a wrinkled sheet out and handed it to Hazel. "I see," said Hazel.

The girl started nibbling at what was left of her thumbnail. "Can we still do it?" she asked.

"Are you having a hard time remembering?" asked Hazel. "Pandora can be a bit stubborn at times."

"I don't know," said the girl. "I attributed it to writer's block."

"Well, maybe you should tell me what happened in West Liberty again. We can try to use that as a springboard for the reading."

"On the afternoon of September 13th," the girl recounted, "I saw a flyer in Memorial Union announcing a Día de Independencia fiesta in West Liberty on Sunday the 15th. I thought it would be interesting to see how Midwestern Mexican Americans celebrate Mexican Independence Day, so I rode my bike out there and found out. I was more than a little surprised to see Old Glory hanging next to the Mexican flag there in the 4-H Club, and when they opened the festivities with the 'The Star Spangled Banner' instead of the Mexican national anthem (which they played *after* 'The Star-Spangled Banner'), I knew it wasn't the kind of Independencia fiesta that the people of Juárez would've understood."

"And what did you see at this fiesta that reminded you of your dream?" Hazel asked, trying to steer the girl back on track.

"A piñata," said the girl, "an old-fashioned, star-shaped piñata almost exactly like the one in my dream."

"Explain 'star-shaped piñata,' " said Hazel. "I'm not up to date on Mexican culture."

"Neither am I," said the girl, "but I do know that they don't make star-shaped piñatas any more, at least not in Juárez. The ones they sell at the mercado look like burros and Superman, but my grandpa told me that when he was a kid, and even when my mom was a kid, the piñatas in those days were stars: round in the middle with papier-mâché cones sticking out and crepe paper tassels hanging off the tips of the cones."

The girl unclipped her fountain pen from her blouse and scratched out a drawing of the piñata on the wrinkled essay sheet.

"The round part was actually a clay pot covered up with colored crepe paper," the girl's exegesis continued, "and this is where the candy was, as well as fruits and nuts and little toys. You see, piñatas used to be used only for Christmas, that's what my grandpa told me, and that's why they were so beautiful and so special, and they were shaped like stars to symbolize the Star of Bethlehem. Now they use piñatas mainly for birthdays and also for some special holidays, but I've never seen a star-shaped piñata except for in my dream. And then to see one in West Liberty, Iowa, of all places! Talk about authentic freak-out!"

"You said this piñata in West Liberty was 'almost exactly' like the one in your dream," Hazel reminded her. "What was the difference?"

"Why don't I just tell you the dream?" the girl said. "You do want to hear the story of the dream, don't you?"

"Of course," said Hazel. "Let me get myself set up." She opened the teakwood box and took out a tiny tape recorder. "Ready," she said, pressing the REC button.

The girl had a suspicious look in her eye. "You didn't say anything about taping the session," she said.

"Since we've agreed that you're going to let me use your dream in the book I'm writing," said Hazel, "that's what the waiver you signed was all about—"

"I thought you meant your interpretation of it," the girl put in, "not the whole dream, word for word. It's like it won't belong to me any more just because I don't have to pay you for this reading."

Hazel pulled her glasses off and rubbed her eyes. "Look, you can back out of the agreement if it makes you feel better," she said. "I didn't realize you wanted to copyright your dream."

"I'm a writer," said the girl. "I might do that."

Hazel hooked her glasses back on. ""Fine," she said. "When we're done, I'll give you the tape. But it's important to have the dream on tape in case you make any allusions or drop any clues or have any flashes of insight as you're telling it to me. Those nuances and innuendoes of the moment might hold the seeds of the real meaning. Shall we proceed?"

"Okay, I'm about eight or nine in this dream," the girl began suddenly, "and my mom is dressing me up to go to a birthday party across the border in Juárez. I've got this white dress on, real shiny material, like satin, with a blue satin bow at the back of my waist and another one on my head. I'm also wearing white gloves and white patent leather shoes; it feels like I'm going to a Holy Communion instead of a birthday party. I'm not too thrilled about going to this party. It's not just my clothes that make me uncomfortable; it's something else that I never remember at this point in the dream. But my mom is making me go, kind of dragging me there, actually.

"We have to go across the bridge, as I said, because this party is in Juárez, but it's not happening at anybody's house. The piñata is right there on the levee of the Rio Grande. I can see the piñata hanging between two trees as we come over the bridge and look down past the Tortilla Curtain.

"Anyway, we go through the turnstile and then go around the corner at the Mexican customs building and head towards the colonias, the poorest section of Juárez, which is directly across the river from the university. As we're walking along the riverbank, I can hear all the kids at the party screaming and laughing, rattling on in Spanish, and I begin to realize in the dream that this is part of what makes me uncomfortable about coming to this party. Everybody's speaking Spanish, and I can't speak Spanish very well. (This is not just part of the dream. I really do have a gringa accent from having gone to school on the El Paso side all my life and not being allowed to speak Spanish at any of those schools.) So I decide not to talk or play with anybody at this party. I feel real stupid in this fancy dress, too, because all the other kids look like the little beggars that hang out on the Córdoba bridge.

"As soon as we get to where the piñata's hanging, all the kids get in line to take their turns at breaking it. It's the most incredible piñata

I've ever seen, a giant star made of translucent pink glass that catches the sun and reflects it into rainbows on the dirt of the levee; even the tassels are made of glass, strings of glass beads that sound like little bells in the wind. I don't want to get in line. Not only am I boycotting the party, I also can't believe they want to shatter that glass star. It seems holy to me, but not holy in a peaceful way like the Virgin Mary, holy in a scary way, like when a penitent whips himself in a Holy Week procession.

"I tell my mom I don't want to stay at this party. That I'm scared and want to go home, but she tells me I have to get in line and take my turn like all the other kids, that it's rude if we leave before the piñata has been broken. She pulls a handkerchief out of her pocket and blindfolds me. I try to pull away from her. I tell her I'm at the end of the line—how come she's putting a blindfold on me if it's not even my turn yet? She tells me everybody's got to wear a blindfold. Nobody can see this piñata being broken, she says, because the glass might get into your eyes and blind you.

"She leaves me standing there, with the blindfold so tight I can feel the knot digging into the back of my head. I call out to her not to leave me alone, that I'm scared because I know I'm gonna get punished if I break this piñata, but she tells me over and over: *No tengas miedo, Xochitl. Don't be afraid, Xochitl.* (My first name is Xochitl, which is an Aztec name, but my mom told me that the priest wouldn't baptize me unless I had a Christian name to go along with it, so they named me Xochitl María, and the nuns started calling me Mary in the first grade.)

"Anyway, the line is moving quickly. Nobody's even hit a cone on the piñata. You only get three swings when it's your turn, and if you don't hit anything in those three swings, then you pass the stick to the next kid and the next kid, until finally somebody breaks it and all the candy falls out. That's when everybody goes wild.

"All of a sudden, a pair of hands starts turning me around to make me dizzy, so I know it's my turn to swing at the piñata. I keep seeing the image of that glass star in my head, that holy symbol of something I don't understand. I call out to my mom again, but she keeps telling me not to be afraid, that she promises I won't get punished. Then the stick is in my hands, and I'm so scared I start pissing my pants; I can feel it running down the inside of my legs and into my socks. The other kids are chanting *Quiébrala! Quiébrala!* Break it! Break it!

"And then all these hands are at my back, pushing me closer and closer to the piñata, and I turn around to threaten them with my stick, yelling *'I want to go home! Let me go home!'* I swing the stick back to hit those hands that are pushing me, and then I hear the shattering behind me. I have killed the glass piñata. I have sinned.

"I always wake up terrified. I don't know why I keep having this dream, but I tell you, seeing that star-shaped piñata in West Liberty scared me so much I cried.

"The funny thing is, though, that my mom hated Mexico. She was from there, from the interior, but she hated talking about it, and she never wanted to go across the bridge to the mercado or the bullfights with my dad and me. She used to say there was too much pain in Mexico, and that she couldn't stand remembering the pain. She *never* would've taken me to a party in the colonias."

The girl took a deep breath and sighed as she exhaled. She took off her cap and tousled her short hair. Hazel clicked off the tape recorder.

"When did you lose your mother?" asked Hazel.

The girl looked Hazel straight in the eye. "My mom killed herself four years ago," she said in a cold voice. "She shot up too much insulin and gave herself a heart attack."

Hazel raised her eyebrows but didn't say anything. She opened the box again and took out the silk-wrapped Morgan-Greer deck. "What I want you to do now," she said, unwrapping the deck slowly, "is to go through the tarot and choose five cards that will represent the five most important images in your dream. Then spread them out on the table, following the sequence the images had in the dream. Understand?" She set the deck face down in front of the girl. The girl nodded.

"I'll be back in fifteen minutes," Hazel said. "I know what it feels like to lose a parent at that age."

The girl nodded again, but she was staring at the stars on the back of the top card. Hazel left her alone and went to brew a fresh pot of coffee. On the way in, she noticed the sky had a violet tint to it. It was the end of Indian summer all right.

"We may have to come inside. Looks like a storm," she called to the girl, but the girl was wiping her eyes with the sleeve of her blouse. The storm had already started. Hazel opened the screen door that led to her kitchen. She needed to write down her first thoughts on this piñata dream. What an archetype!

III

The memory had slipped down from her forehead like the eyes of the Black Angel:

"*Come help Mami, Xochitl. The tea's almost ready.*"

The pungent odor of the boiling herbs hung like tar in the kitchen, the vapor clinging to Mary's skin.

"*Get the honey,*" her mom would say, and Mary would dig the measuring spoon into the honey and draw out two tablespoons for the tea that her mom was straining into a clay cup. It was Mary's job to stir the tea until all the honey dissolved. Her mom got the needle ready. Mary held her breath as her mom sat on the chair, lifted her skirt, rolled down her stockings, and shot the insulin into both thighs.

"*I'm going to lie down on your bed, Xochitl. Don't forget to bring me the tea in fifteen minutes to help Mami come out of her trance.*" Always the same words.

Mary would wait just outside the bedroom door, eyes glued to the second hand of her watch, afraid of thinking, terrified her dad would come home early, or her grandpa would stop by with a bag of groceries. Only she and her mom could know about this secret ritual. If anybody else found out that her mom was putting herself into trances to speak to the Virgin face to face, the Virgin would punish her mom and take her life away. So Mary guarded the secret as carefully as she counted the 900 seconds.

Mary tried to make the memory roll back into her head so that she could concentrate on finding the five cards. She turned the deck over and looked at the first card. A naked man and woman standing in a garden like Adam and Eve. Not that one. She turned to the next card. A skeleton in a black-hooded cape holding a scythe. She set that card on the table. Three more cards and then she came upon one with a big, orange sun that reminded her of the piñata. She laid that card beside the other one. Eight more cards and she found one with a blindfolded woman. This one for sure. The next card made her set the whole deck down. The devil was staring at her through a goat's head. She went to the next card, and the next, and the next, then looked back at the devil card, then moved forward again, counting.

She passed twenty-five cards. The twenty-sixth one showed five hands holding five sticks. All the hands pushing her to hit the piñata, she thought, placing the card beside the blindfolded woman.

She needed one more card, but she couldn't figure out which important image she had left out. She looked at the four cards on the table and realized that the missing image was the border. She combed through the rest of the deck and found only one card that could, with some imagination, represent the border. It had eight branches slanted over the top and at the bottom, a blue river separating two pieces of green land.

She started ordering the cards but felt raindrops pattering on the back of her neck. She heard the squeaky hinges of the screen door.

"I knew it!" called Hazel, running across the lawn. "We better hurry! These autumn storms . . ." The rest of her sentence was dispersed in the wind. She tossed the tape recorder and the tarot deck into the box. Mary shielded the five cards with her backpack as she followed Hazel into the house. The sky was a purple bruise, and the wind whipped the yellow branches of the weeping willow in the yard. Mary shuddered as another memory echoed in her head. *Don't go to the levee, Xochitl. La Llorona hides in the weeping willows on the levee. She's a kidnapper.*

"Just made it!" said Hazel as the downpour drenched the boards of the back stoop. "Have a seat. Coffee's ready." She pointed to the bay window where the table and chairs were nearly buried in a jungle of African violets. The rain sluiced off the windowpanes. Mary pulled a chair out, and a tabby cat peered up at her through emerald eyes.

"That's Athena," said Hazel, setting two mugs on the table. "Move over, Athena."

The cat uncurled itself and sprang off the chair. Mary slipped into the warm seat.

"Any luck with the cards?" asked Hazel, pouring the coffee from a percolator.

"I just have to put them in order," Mary said as Hazel dragged her chair to sit beside her. Mary held the cards like a poker hand and moved them in and out of different slots until she had the right order. "This is easier than I thought," she said. "Like putting a story into pictures." She laid the cards before Hazel one by one.

"Here's the setting," she explained, "but you have to pretend the river and the land are brown instead of green and blue like that. El Paso's in the desert."

"Which side is El Paso in this card?" asked Hazel.

"The one with the castle," said Mary without any doubt. The castle was her house in Sunset Heights.

"I thought so," said Hazel. She held her mug under her nose and inhaled the steam of the coffee.

"The piñata's the conflict," said Mary. "Here's the main character. All these hands are the obstacles. And this is the denouement. See what I mean? It's a perfect story."

Hazel sipped on her coffee as she studied the cards. "The tarot makes things so clear," she said.

"Interpret," said Mary.

"I'm going to talk about the meaning of the spread first," Hazel told her. "Then we'll associate the story of the spread with the story of your dream, okay?"

"I'm ready," said Mary. She could feel her pulse beating in her neck.

"The opening card tells us what the issue is," Hazel began, "and you've opened with the Eight of Rods. Rods are the suit that represents the Self, particularly the Self-concept, the identity." She took another sip from her mug.

Mary tasted the coffee, found it too bitter, and pushed the mug aside.

"The Eight of Rods tells us that you are in the process of regrouping your Self-concept. You're analyzing your identity, trying to determine who you are."

"Everybody's doing that," said Mary.

"True," said Hazel, "in some form or another, we are all engaged in that process, but remember, you picked this card, and you chose to open the spread with it; this means your process, your awareness of the process, is probably your first priority right now, though you may not realize it. You also may not realize you have a guide." She tapped the Sun card. "This is your guide, your beacon, the star that you should follow. The Sun is a universal symbol of life, but in the tarot, it also implies an inner journey that will enrich your life. It could be a spiritual journey, or a quest for the Self, even a physical trip or vacation. What the Sun card means is that you should embark on your journey, whatever it is; it is a bright time to go."

Hazel poured herself another cup of coffee. The storm rattled the windows.

"Any questions so far?" asked Hazel. Mary shook her head, rubbing her hands to warm them. Under the table, the cat grazed Mary's leg.

"Swords," Hazel continued, pointing to the card of the blindfolded woman, "represent the conscious mind, the conscious awareness. Obviously, our main character here doesn't want to be aware of something. The blindfold indicates that she doesn't want to see, she doesn't want to be conscious of this questioning of her identity. She's got two swords in her hands, which represent two options she must choose between, and she could use these swords to remove the blindfold. But, you see, removing the blindfold is the equivalent of making the choice, and she can only make the choice if she's aware of the options, but she doesn't want to be responsible for that. So the blindfold stays."

"I should be making an outline of this," said Mary, reaching down to take a notebook out of her pack.

"Now we move on to the Five of Rods," said Hazel, "another identity card. This one tells us that you are already experiencing changes inside yourself, even though you aren't aware of the causes. Changes, of course, bring conflicts; that's why all the hands look like they're engaged in a brawl. You could say that each rod in each hand represents a different aspect of your identity, aspects that are not very compatible right now, and that are manifesting themselves in a kind of chaos."

Mary scribbled "identity chaos" in her notebook.

Hazel twirled her mug between her hands before going on to the Death card. Athena rubbed against Mary's leg again.

"Your cat's making me nervous," Mary said.

"Athena, get out of here!" said Hazel, but Athena curled herself under the table and kept her green gaze on Mary's ankles.

"The good thing about chaos," Hazel continued, "is that it always leads to catharsis. The denouement, as you called the Death card, is a very positive card here, but you probably chose it for its negative connotations, right? Probably to symbolize how afraid you were at having 'killed the glass piñata,' as you put it."

"What's positive about death?" said Mary.

"The Death card doesn't always mean physical death," explained Hazel, "especially not in this context. The Death card simply means an end to something. This spread has shown us that the something involves your identity, your quest for self-definition, a journey that's creating havoc right now, mainly because you can't see what your options are. The Death card tells us that the chaos will end if you choose to remove the blindfold. The outcome of the journey will be the death of confusion, which means the birth of clarity. You see, the

Death card is really an indicator of rebirth. The scythe in the skeleton's hand is a harvest tool, and the crop to be harvested is the inner self."

Mary picked up her mug and swallowed some of the cold, bitter coffee. "This is what my dream means?" she asked.

"Associatively speaking, yes," said Hazel. "Let me just ask you a couple of questions before I give you the punch line. First, exactly when had you start having this dream?"

"I don't remember," said Mary. "A long time ago."

"How long? What grade were you in? Was your mother still alive?"

Mary's mouth opened. She looked at Hazel, then down at the cards, then back at Hazel. "No," she said. "It started the same day my mom died. We were riding in my grandpa's car back from the funeral, and I fell asleep against his arm and had that dream."

"That would explain the birthday party," said Hazel. "Pandora often gives us images that seem opposite to each other. The other side of death is birth; the other side of a funeral would be a birthday party."

"But it wasn't my *mom's* birthday," said Mary.

"Maybe it was *your* birthday," Hazel suggested. "Maybe that's why you're all dressed up and why you're the one who has to break the piñata. After the funeral, you probably felt that a part of you had died, and indeed it had, but that death signified the birth of something else. The birth of a new identity, perhaps."

"What new identity?" asked Mary.

Hazel crossed her legs into a lotus position on the chair. "Wait," she said, "tell me about the flowers."

Mary felt ice cubes sliding down her back. "What flowers? The funeral flowers?" she said.

"These flowers," said Hazel. "All the sunflowers on the Sun card and the white rose on the Death card. What do they have to do with your dream?"

"I didn't even pay any attention to those," said Mary. "I was going for the major images in the cards."

"*You* may not have been paying attention," Hazel smiled, "but Pandora was. The sunflowers, for example, symbolize fertility, the fertility given by the sun, the ripening of your conscious mind, the seeds of awareness. In other words, the sunflowers contain the seeds of your new identity. And the white rose here, is you, blooming on the Death card. Didn't you say you were dressed all in white in this dream?"

Mary stared at the pink and purple blooms of the African violets on the table, at the downy stems that were so different from the thorny stem of the white rose. "Oh my god," she gasped. "My last name, Espinosa, means thorny one."

Hazel clenched her fist and looked up at the ceiling. "Thank you, Pandora," she said. "What does your other name mean? The Aztec one?"

"Xochitl? I don't know. I never asked."

Hazel uncrossed her legs. "Okay, here's my interpretation of your dream," she said, pausing slightly for a dramatic effect that brought Mary to the edge of her chair.

"You are at *Xochitl's* birthday party," said Hazel, "which is happening on the most impoverished side of your psychic border, the Mexican side of your identity. And you're dressed for a communion ceremony because, in effect, you are going to commune with Xochitl, the mysterious one, the part of you that you've repressed because she represents negative things like your mother's pain, or poverty, or not fitting in.

"But Xochitl lives inside the piñata. I'm interpreting the star-shaped piñata as a symbol for Mexico. And the piñata holds this mysterious identity of yours that you're afraid to see because of its negative connotations. But remember, the blindfolded woman has a choice to make: you can continue to see Xochitl in a negative light, or you can take off the blindfold and see her in the light of this glass piñata. Either way, you're going to break the piñata. That's Pandora's way of telling you that you need to confront this issue on a conscious level. And the Death card suggests that at the end of the process, you will experience a rebirth."

"You mean I, as Mary, am going to die, and I, as Xochitl, am going to be reborn?" Mary asked, frowning. "What do I have to do, change my name and move to Mexico?"

"I mean Xochitl and Mary will become one," said Hazel. "You don't have to go to any extremes for that to happen, but maybe you should find out who Xochitl is. What's her history? What's her genealogy? What does her name mean? Pandora already knows all this, but she won't release the information until you're ready to commune with Xochitl, and what better way than to communicate through the medium of your own writing? You told me on Saturday that writing is your truth. If you infuse that truth with Xochitl's spirit, I think you could achieve a true balance between the two sides of your identity. And that's when you would experience your rebirth."

Rebirth. Truth. Spirit. Balance.

Platitudes, that's what all this was. New Age bullshit platitudes!

"This is bullshit," she said to Hazel, although she could not understand why she had suddenly started to cry. Why suddenly all her bones ached, and her heart felt as though it had been ripped out by the roots.

"I feel like I've been sacrificed," said Mary, wiping her nose with the inside of her wrist.

Hazel put her hand on Mary's shoulder. "It's a lot to deal with, I know," said Hazel. "This is the way these trips to Pandora's Jungle usually turn out the first time."

"I have to go," said Mary. She reached down for her backpack and found Athena sprawled on it. She laughed in spite of the tears, and then the crying got worse, and the tears just sluiced off Mary's face.

"Let me get you a tissue," said Hazel, but Mary picked up her pack and headed for the back door.

"Isn't your bike out front?" asked Hazel, and Mary realized she'd forgotten about her bike, which she'd left standing against the side of the house and was probably blowing down to the Iowa River by now. Again, Mary laughed, a repressed hysterical kind of laughing that hurt her chest as she stumbled out of the kitchen and to the hallway where she found her bike. Hazel's roommate had probably brought it in. Mary lifted the stand with her heel and walked the ten-speed out the door. Outside, she could not distinguish between her tears and the rain that blurred her vision.

When she got home, her clothes were a second skin, and her teeth chattered so loudly it gave her a headache. She had not stopped crying. The only thing she wanted was to hide. She scribbled a note to her roommate to please not disturb her and to tell whoever called her on the phone that she was hiding and couldn't talk to anybody. Then, she took a hot shower and crawled into the flannel sheets. She cried the way she had not cried since her mom's funeral.

Late in the afternoon, she remembered her poetry class but knew there was no way she could go. She got up and put a tape on, then lay in bed listening to the tolling of bells and the somber chanting of Benedictine monks. The rain had not stopped.

She was not aware of hunger or thirst. Apart from the chanting and the rain beating on the window, she heard only one thing: *No tengas miedo, Xochitl. Don't be afraid, Xochitl.* She covered her head with the sheet and curled herself up like Athena, letting her tears and saliva soak into the futon.

She awoke to a great silence within her. When she surfaced from under the covers, she saw that her room was drenched in moonlight. The storm had passed. In the next room, her roommate was pecking at the typewriter. She got up, turned the lamp on over her bookshelf, and reached for her English translation of the *Popul-Vuh*.

IV

Dear Hazel,

Today is November 2nd, and in Mexico that means it's the Day of the Dead, an appropriate day for me to be writing this. I have been digging up Aztec history in the library, and I thought you would like to know (although, apparently, Pandora already knows) that the name Xochitl means flower.

I also wanted to tell you that I'm sorry I acted like a brat about your using the piñata dream in your book. I hope it serves your purposes as well as it served me.

Thank you so much for introducing me to Pandora. She's been tossing up one memory after another, so many at a time that I often feel as though I'm living in a twilight zone surrounded by glass piñatas. I still don't know what my earliest remembered dream is, but I've swung the stick at my earliest memory, and this is what came out:

I'm in the first grade, and I can't remember the "Pledge of Allegiance," so I just move my lips and look up at the flag. But Sister Catherine—the one who started calling me Mary—is standing behind me snapping a ruler in her hand. When the "Pledge" is finished, she tells me to take the ruler and hit myself on the mouth for lying, for pretending to know the words of the "Pledge." I do as she tells me, and then she announces to the class that I'm not a real American because I can't say the "Pledge of Allegiance," and she says that I don't even deserve to look at the American flag. For the rest of first grade, my desk faced the back of the classroom. And Sister Catherine always had me wait in the hall while the rest of the class said the "Pledge of Allegiance."

Manifest Destiny strikes again!!

One more thing. Ever since we broke the piñata dream, incredible stories—part memory, part fantasy—have been breaking out of me. I've dropped my poetry workshop as it's been a bad influence on my writing. I'm almost finished with the stories, and I'd like for you to read them. Interested? They are mainly about my mom and her past. Some of the information came from my dad, some from research, and the rest from some wild corner of my imagination. I don't know if I've infused my writing with Xochitl's spirit, as you advised, but they are definitely more Xochitl's stories than Mary's. I owe their existence to Pandora.

Gracias,
Xochitl María Espinosa

Xochitl's Stories

Estrella González

It was said that Estrella González had no past, that she had always been as she was, a wise woman, a healer, and a worker of magic. That, in 1891, when my great grandfather Joaquín (Don Abuelo) was just a boy, she had appeared one evening in his village riding on a mule. With nothing in her possession but a blanket and a snakeskin medicine bag, she proclaimed that from the next day forward, the village of San Martincito would have both a new name and a new curandera. The new name, she announced, would be La Subida de Las Almas. She had been traveling for many months in search of the pueblo where she would fulfill her destiny, the place marked in her star chart as The Rising of the Souls, and had at last come upon San Martincito.

"This village has been chosen as the entrance to the land of the dead," she explained. "And I, Estrella González, was sent to protect you. What good is a curandero who cannot speak to you and tell you of all the changes that will befall, a curandero who cannot hear your fears and sorrows? A healer's power is the power to live inside the patient's skin, to see and feel and hear as you do. The power to know Change and prepare for it when it happens. How can you give your faith to one whose power is locked inside him? You must start over again. Tomorrow, your new life begins."

Then, as suddenly as she had arrived, she turned her mule around and rode back into the jungle of prickly pears from which she had emerged.

There had been another healer then, a deaf-mute named Ciriaco whose family had served the village for hundreds of years. Nobody could understand how the strange woman, Estrella González, knew about Ciriaco and his affliction, but the morning after her visit, it was discovered that Ciriaco had disappeared, his house empty except for the scorpions walking over his hammock. And the rumor spread that the new curandera was to blame, that she was a black witch and had brought a plague of scorpions into the village.

A priest was sent for from the nearby town of Ejutla, but when the priest gathered the men and sent them out to hunt for the bruja, arming them with torches and machetes and their wives' rosaries, they found no sign of her. No trail of hoof prints, no trace of a path or a shelter. She had ridden up into the foothills and vanished.

So the men stopped mining in those hills for fear the bruja would cast a spell and make them disappear, and they never tried to hunt for her again, despite the priest's warning that God would punish them if they allowed an hechicera to live.

For nine years, Estrella González did not show herself to the people, but she left signs to let them know that she was there. Sometimes, a bright, blue-green parrot would perch on the thatched roofs of the chozas, squawking in a language that nobody remembered. At other times, the men would discover their fishing nets floating in the middle of the bay or down in the well, and the women would suddenly notice that their washboards were gone, that the cornmeal for their tortillas had been taken.

There was a meadow in San Martincito covered with flax and fed by a spring that ran under the earth. It was because of this flax that the women of the village had earned a name for themselves as master weavers. With the thread they spun from the fibers of the plant, they wove pale gold rebozos of the finest linen, which the men sold or exchanged for livestock in Oaxaca. When the meadow started drying up, the flax plants dropping their flowers like blue lace, everyone knew that the priest's prediction had come true.

The people watched the pattern of their lives loosen from the warp of tradition, the woof falling away like rotted thread. The meadow became a wasteland, and the waistlooms for the rebozos gathered dust in the corners of the huts. Now the women made baskets and cloth dolls to sell, and the men had to trade their fish for twine and blankets. The weavers of San Martincito faded into the past, along with Ciriaco, pulling with them the pride and the spirit of the village itself.

When my great grandfather was sixteen, a meeting was called to discuss the future of the village. The young men wanted to decide upon a name. They were tired, they said, of not knowing what to call themselves, especially when they accompanied their fathers to market. They were embarrassed to say they were from San Martincito, for the rumors had carried even to the city that the people of San Martincito were hechizados, and nobody would buy the wares of a cursed village.

Don Abuelo led the motion to adopt the name the bruja had given them. La Subida de Las Almas was not a bad name, he said, though he admitted to not knowing what it meant. Perhaps just La Subida would be good.

"At least it doesn't sound like San Martincito," he argued, "and we could specialize in a new trade. There is plenty of wood; we could become carvers or carpenters. In a few years, nobody will even remember the linen shawls of San Martincito, or the curse, and we can start over again, just like la vieja esa said."

When their masks and crucifixes, at first carved with an intricate vengeance on the curandera, became almost as popular as their rebozos had been, some said that Estrella González had at last left them alone. They could work and live in peace again, they said, and be the dictators of their own fates. But others felt indebted to Estrella González: those who remembered that their milpas had never yielded as much corn, nor the sea as much fish, and those who found that the women had never been as fertile, nor the fruit trees, nor the chickens. But it was Don Abuelo's mother, Hortensia, who realized that, in the nine years they had lived under La Vieja's influence, not one child, not one animal, had become ill. Everyone had been too busy blaspheming Estrella González to notice that her influence on their lives had brought an end to sickness.

"Losing our curandero was not a great tragedy," she reminded them at another of their meetings, "because none of us has needed a healer in nine years. I think we have La Vieja to thank for that. So what if she changed everything? Most of us are still here, and our children are stronger and healthier than ever. We can't let our rancor blind us to that."

A murmur of assent rose among the women. Hortensia's comadre, Brígida, pointed out that, in spite of her own hatred of Estrella González, she had to admit she was thankful that none of her family had gotten sick.

"I heard the dengue hit Acapulco again this year," Brígida told them. "That bug hasn't touched us in nine years. Remember what a fever the dengue gave? I almost lost my little Chayo from that damn bug!"

"Not only that," cried Hortensia, "look what's happening all over the Republic. The campesinos have lost the land, thanks to that desgraciado Díaz, but nobody's taken anything away from us. I tell you, Estrella González is protecting this village, and I, for one, am going to thank her with a basket of maíz!"

"But you can't go up there, Hortensia," her husband scolded. "If la vieja esa does live there, she'll curse you for sure."

"¡Ay!" Hortensia spat at the ground. "I've had enough of curses. Tell me, Pancho, is it a curse that your son isn't dying of the dengue fever? That your lands are still yours? If it is, then I hope we're cursed forever!"

Hortensia got the women organized, and each of them sent a gift of thanks up to Estrella González. Hortensia picked the best ears of corn; Brígida took wax for candles and chocolate; and there were baskets of squash and figs, fresh-made tortillas wrapped up in fine cloth, strings of dried fish, clay bowls, even an old waistloom that one of the younger women donated, along with a spool of linen thread, probably the last linen thread in the village.

Of course, Pancho was furious, as were the rest of the old men, but secretly, Joaquín was very pleased. *At last*, he thought, *we are going to come out of the shadow of hatred*. He set himself to carving the best crucifix he'd ever made. When his mother and three of the braver women set off into the foothills, it was Joaquín who led the burro (the poor thing could barely walk with all those baskets tied to his back), and, when he knew they were out of the eyesight of the village, he gave his mother the crucifix and told her it was his gift of gratitude for La Vieja. He dared not give it to Estrella González himself for fear the news would reach his father, and he and the other men would turn their backs on Joaquín for being a traitor.

"My mother was an incredible woman," Don Abuelo said sadly. "She understood perfectly; in fact, she even pretended that I'd said something offensive to her and sent me back to the village with a good whack on the head. When the story reached my father, as I knew it would, that I had insulted the curandera, he patted me on the back and said, 'I wouldn't have expected anything less, hijo. We have to stick together. Can't let those women order us around.'

"But you know what?" Don Abuelo continued, squinting hard, as if to see far back into the crevices of his memory, "Do you know what my mother told me that night after Papá had gone to sleep? I was outside singing to the moon and tuning my guitar, and she came up behind me and laid her sweet hand on my head. In the silence just before she spoke, I could hear that she was weeping. I heard the sniffle and the long, trembling breath she took from deep within her stomach.

" 'I saw her, Joaquín,' she said. 'The others were too afraid to wait for her to show up. After we unpacked the baskets and laid them in front of a kind of grotto that we found up there, they all picked up their skirts and came back running. But I stayed. I hid behind a clump of nopales and waited until I saw her. I had to see her, you understand. I had to believe she was really there.

" 'I didn't have to wait very long. She must have been watching from somewhere, just waiting for everyone to leave. I don't know, maybe she knew I was hiding and didn't care, maybe she was just curious, but she appeared after a little while, riding on her mule again. Remember that, Joaquín? That skinny mule of hers and that snakeskin morral? She hadn't changed much, except she seemed . . . how can I put it? . . . *normal*, like a normal human being wondering what her neighbors are up to.

" 'She stood over the baskets and just stared at everything. I don't know if she was confused or humiliated or what, but her face, Joaquín, her face just looked so sad. Such suffering in that face. I wanted to jump up and put my arms around her and beg for her forgiveness. I felt so guilty for all of us. And then you know what she did, hijo? You know the only thing she took?

" 'I'd torn the whiskers off some of the corn, just enough to make a nice little bed for your crucifix. I didn't want to lay it on the bare ground, but it wasn't right to put it with anybody else's gift, either. And it looked so beautiful, hijo, the Christ's face and the body were so elegant, so well carved. Your crucifix is all she took, son, corn silk and all. She put it in her apron, then she climbed back on her mule and rode away, leaving all that food to rot in the sun.' "

Don Abuelo always paused at this spot in the story and rolled a cigarette. His fingers trembled, and when he smoked, the strip of ash at the end of the cigarette flaked over his knuckles. Through the thick, green glasses that he wore even at night, I could see his eyes shining. I had to be careful not to seem impatient. I couldn't ask him any questions or goad him for any details, otherwise he would simply shake his head and say he'd wasted enough time in tonterías. But, if I sat perfectly still and didn't intrude upon his memories, the story would soon flow out again, enveloping us both like rings of smoke.

Hortensia went to the grotto several times after that first visit. Joaquín didn't know what she did up there, what made her keep going back. Pancho became angry and suspicious, and finally he just stopped talking to Hortensia altogether. With Joaquín, Pancho was always kind, but he knew his son was on Hortensia's side, or at least he knew Joaquín understood Hortensia's fascination with Estrella González. Joaquín never reproached her for being gone or for not having the comida ready when they returned from the fields, even when his father insisted that he do so.

"It is your mother's obligation to be here, taking care of her house, feeding her son and husband. Instead, she's off climbing hills and taking presents to an old witch that's ruined all our lives. You better tell her, Joaquín. You better warn her that she's looking for trouble if she keeps this up."

But Pancho knew Joaquín would never tell Hortensia anything. He knew his son was on her side.

One Sunday, Hortensia woke Joaquín very early. The stars were still out, but he could hear the morning tide starting to wash up on the beach. She told him that she had to leave and didn't know what time she would return.

"I think La Vieja is going to let me speak to her today," she whispered. "I don't know how long I'll have to wait, but I can feel it, son. I'm going to speak to her, and I'll wait as long as I have to. You understand, don't you, Joaquín?"

"Take me with you, Mamá," Joaquín said. "I want to meet her and hear her speak."

"But what about your father? He'll never trust you again. Nobody will; not the men, at least. I don't think you'll gain anything, son. The people here can be very cruel."

"It's funny," Don Abuelo mused, stroking the white stubble of his beard, "how suddenly, out of some dark corner of your mind, you can see your destiny opening up like a clear path in a jungle. Suddenly you know what it is you have to do, and you don't care what the consequences are going to be. No other lesson is ever more important than that. That morning, I knew I had to go with Mamá. I had to stop being a hypocrite."

He dressed quickly and fed the burro and the chickens while Hortensia wrote a note to Pancho, which Joaquín read just before they left.

> *Your son has gone with me. He is not defying you, he loves you very much, but we all have to obey God's will, Pancho, and it is God's will that Joaquín go with me today. Please try to understand. Your son's destiny is something you cannot control.*

As soon as they stepped out of the house, and that brisk ocean breeze hit Joaquín's face, he knew he was doing the right thing, the only thing, and that he was going to be changed after this experience. Hortensia had to tell him several times to settle down. He was behaving like a schoolboy, jumping around, whistling, throwing rocks. He kept chattering about how lucky he felt, how he was going to buy a full page of lottery tickets and get Hortensia a sewing machine and his father a team of horses with the million pesos he was going to win.

"Here, have some piloncillo and be quiet," Hortensia told him, handing him a hard piece of molasses from the basket she carried on her head. "We're not going to a quinceañera, you know. This is a solemn day."

She was right, of course, and Joaquín had to force himself to keep still. The walk seemed very long to him and to keep from talking, he asked his mother to tell about her other visits.

"Have you actually let La Vieja see you? Weren't you afraid, Mamá?"

"Afraid of what? A poor, lonely woman with nothing but prickly pears for neighbors? Nonsense. I bet she's more afraid of me than I am of her."

"What does she do, Mamá? What keeps you coming back here?"

"She gets to the grotto just as the sun starts to show itself over the water. From our hiding place, we'll be able to see the sea in the distance and what used to be the meadow on the outskirts of the village. You'll see that it's nothing but desert now, full of snakes and scorpions, I'm sure, but just as the sun rises, a miracle happens, hijo. The meadow comes back just for an instant! Remember the long, green grass you used to roll in while I picked the flax for my weaving and that rich, black dirt that you couldn't keep your hands out of? And all those blue flowers. Remember, hijo? It comes back."

"And then what happens, Mamá? What's La Vieja doing?"

"She's dancing," Hortensia said simply, as if there were nothing else in the world for the old woman to be doing. "She's naked, and she's got a great big perico perched on one shoulder, and her hair hangs down her back in black waves. She's whirling around and around the grotto like a top spinning in the dirt."

They had finally reached the small clearing at the top of the hill where the grotto stood, and Joaquín saw that it was built of river stones piled on top of each other against the wide trunk of a ceiba tree. Hortensia took her basket of piloncillo and set it at the foot of the grotto, then she hurried back to where Joaquín crouched behind a giant nopal.

"What's in there?" Joaquín asked, wanting to go and look inside the grotto, certain that there would be brujería dolls nailed to the tree or dead iguanas hanging by their tails.

"None of your business," Hortensia told him. "Just turn around and wait for the meadow to appear."

"But I wanted to see La Vieja dancing."

"I told you, she's naked. It would be disrespectful for you to see her like that. Besides, her dancing is a woman's costumbre, meant only for women's eyes."

Joaquín stared down at the mist that had once veiled the famous meadow of San Martincito, feeling cheated, seeing how untrue it was that men were the masters, that men had any kind of power over women. He was so immersed in his self-pity that he would have missed the miracle had Hortensia not tapped him on the leg.

"She's here," Hortensia whispered, and in that instant, with the sunrise shimmering on the mist like a rainbow, Joaquín could see the grassy hillside that he used to tumble down on as a boy; he could see the blue flowers of the flax and the gold light.

"Do you smell that odor, Joaquín?" Hortensia's breath was warm in his ear. "What does it smell like, tell me?"

Joaquín didn't hesitate. He'd been around fishermen all his life. "Viscera," he whispered back. "It's the smell of rotting fish viscera. Something's burning, too. Is she cooking?"

"She's burning copal, the same incense that poor Ciriaco used to burn for his ceremonies, remember? And she's rubbed fish oil all over her body and hair. It must be fish oil; that's why the smell is so strong.

Don't you wonder where she gets her fish, Joaquín? There isn't another village for miles. And that mule of hers wouldn't get her across the sierra."

"Maybe she knows how to fish," said Joaquín, desperate to turn around.

"Can't you see, hijo? She can't go fishing without a boat. The river doesn't have the kind of fish that she uses for that oil of hers; that's the smell of saltwater fish. She gets it from us, from the village. She's got her ways. She wouldn't accept our food when we brought it up to her that one time, remember? And I've brought her more food on my own, but she didn't touch any of it."

"Is she stealing from us, Mamá? Why does she steal from us if we're giving her food?"

"Of course she's not stealing, Joaquín. And she can't accept the food we give her, either. That's charity; she's not here for charity. She's our curandera, our healing woman, and she takes from us because we're supposed to take from her. That we haven't taken from her, that we haven't accepted her as our curandera, is our problem, son. She knows that she's here to stay."

Behind the rasping of his mother's whispers, Joaquín could hear Estrella González dancing. He could hear the creaking of her bones and the wheezing of her lungs. He could even hear the parrot flapping its wings to keep its balance.

"Please let me turn around, Mamá. Just for a second."

"Turn *now*!" Hortensia ordered. "Turn right now and then close your eyes and look back the other way."

Joaquín saw nothing but the grotto and a pair of iridescent blue-green feathers laying on the ground. Estrella González was dancing on the other side of the tree, and Joaquín couldn't see her. Hortensia had tricked him. For the first time in his life, he heard his mother laughing at him.

"Don't make fun of me, Mamá," he said.

"Look!" She nudged him with her elbow. "She's left us a sign. Those two feathers must be a sign that she'll speak to both of us. Come on, Joaquín, we're going to follow her."

Joaquín watched his mother step out of her hiding place and walk past the grotto. He knew he would never go with her. He knew that his fear of Estrella González was just as big as his father's fear and that his father's anger at his mother was just a mask for his cowardice. Joaquín had not come to meet Estrella González; he had not come to hear her speak, but to see whether or not his mother would really go to her. He had imagined he would have to protect Hortensia. He could see it in a headline in the Oaxaca newspaper: *Joaquín Diéguez García Saves His Mother from the Bruja.*

When he saw Hortensia disappear behind the ceiba tree and realized he was alone in that place with the smell of Estrella González, Joaquín put his tail between his legs and was back in the village before his father woke up. He saw the note that Hortensia had left on the table, and he was so ashamed of his own cowardice, and so angry at his mother for not being afraid of Estrella González, that he put the note in his mouth and chewed it into a paste.

Hortensia said later that it was not God's will for Joaquín to meet Estrella González. But she was a wise woman. She knew what had happened to Joaquín. She could see the chicken features in his face. The following month, Joaquín married Doña Brígida's youngest daughter and went north to work for the railroad. He never told the story of Estrella González to anybody. It was his shame and his secret. It wasn't until his grandchildren came along that Joaquín felt brave enough to tell the tale.

The Prediction

When the child appeared in the village naked, bloated, and screaming like a cat in heat, Dionisio Acosta knew that his wife's prayers had been answered. For twelve years, Atizania had made the annual pilgrimage to the Basilica de la Soledad in Oaxaca. Thirty-two kilometers later, her knees like the mashed gizzards of a chicken, Atizania would prostrate herself before the crowned Virgin and pray for the child's arrival. This is not what she told Dionisio she was praying for, but the truth, as always, leaked out, and for twelve years, Dionisio had been using his eyesight with the lust of a doomed bull.

Ciriaco, the deaf-mute curandero of the village, and his mongoloid assistant, Apolonio, came up to where Dionisio was squatting under a fig tree in the plaza weaving a basket.

"Polo is going to marry that girl," said the mongoloid, pointing to the screaming child who did not look more than two years old. Apolonio was twelve.

"Polo has good taste," said Dionisio.

Ciriaco made a series of signs to his assistant and the boy translated. "Ciriaco says that's Atizania's baby."

Dionisio spit a stream of tobacco juice over his shoulder. "I know," he said. Dionisio shaded his eyes and looked in the direction of the well where Atizania, surrounded by Plácida and Berta and a couple of hungry dogs, was already washing the girl's body.

Ciriaco tapped Dionisio's shoulder. Dionisio looked up at him, and Ciriaco pressed his thumb between Dionisio's eyebrows. Apolonio laughed. Dionisio nodded. He didn't need Ciriaco to tell him that the prediction was nearing its climax.

It was a custom in the village that whenever a couple got married, the curandero predicted an important event in their future. For

Dionisio and Atizania the prediction had been that they would not bear children for many years, but that a girl-child would one day appear in the village and come to Atizania. After that, Atizania would grow fertile and Dionisio would go blind.

Dionisio watched Ciriaco and his assistant cross the sunbaked road and approach the women at the well. Ciriaco picked up the child and raised her over his head. He inspected the bottom of her feet and smelled her genitals. He placed her against his chest and felt her bloated, sunburned belly. The child kicked and screamed. (*No doubt the girl has worms*, thought Dionisio.) Ciriaco inspected the girl's toes, and again the girl cried out. Ciriaco gave the child back to Atizania and spoke to Dionisio's wife, his hands moving like wings in the bright light. Apolonio translated. Atizania pressed the girl against her, and the girl rested her head in the crook of Atizania's neck, sucking on the tangerine that Atizania had peeled for her during Ciriaco's examination.

Dionisio turned his attention back to his weaving and decided that this had to be the most beautiful basket he had ever made, probably the last one he would ever see. When Atizania came up to show him the child, Dionisio was tempted to give the girl the evil eye. Maybe if she got sick and died . . . but then, the girl touched his chin, cradling it between her brown, sticky hands, and Dionisio was so ashamed of his selfishness his eyes watered, and he drew the girl to him to hide his face from Atizania. The girl smelled of tangerine and dust and urine. Her brown hair looked like a bird's nest.

"Can she speak?" said Dionisio to his wife.

"She's sick," said Atizania, rubbing the girl's back in circles.

"Worms?"

"Worse. Ciriaco says she's got sugar in the blood. She may not live too long."

Dionisio held the girl at arm's length and looked into her black eyes. The girl frowned. Her nose and cheeks were peeling, as were her shoulders. "She's been out a long time," said Dionisio. "It's a miracle she didn't dehydrate. She must have a strong guardian angel." He tickled the girl under the arms.

"Stop that!" said Atizania. "Tickling isn't good for children. It makes their heart stop."

"I want to see her smile," said Dionisio. "Have you forgotten the second half of the prediction?"

Atizania couldn't meet her husband's eyes. She stared at the little girl's feet. "See those sores between her toes?" she said. "They won't heal because of all the sugar in her blood. That's one of the signs of the disease."

Dionisio picked up one of the girl's legs to examine the sores on her foot. A stream of urine hit him in the face. Dionisio laughed and set her leg down, wiping the urine off with the back of his hand. The girl frowned as she let out the rest of her water. Dionisio had to lift his basket to keep it out of the puddle. "What a stink!" he said, sniffing. "Has this child been drinking mezcal?"

"That's another sign," said Atizania. She untied the bandana from her head and used it to wipe between the girl's legs. "If her urine smells like wet straw, and she's got a bloated belly, and sores that won't heal—those are all signs of the disease. What are we going to do, Nicho?"

Dionisio spit the wad of tobacco behind him, stretched the corners of his mouth with two fingers, and stuck his tongue out at the girl. The girl mimicked him. "Nothing's going to happen to her," said Dionisio. "If she's sick, we'll take care of her. If she dies, we'll bury her. But I don't think she's going to die." He rubbed the girl's head. "Did Ciriaco say anything about this mark?"

Atizania leaned close to the girl and saw that her husband was pointing to a faint brown mark in the shape of scorpion pincers curving just below the girl's hairline on her forehead.

"¡Ay, Virgencita!" said Atizania, crossing herself quickly.

"Wherever this child came from," said Dionisio, reaching up to snap a ripe fig off a low-hanging branch, "she's protected, aren't you, Mercedes?"

"Mercedes?" said Atizania. "I promised the Virgin to call her Soledad."

Dionisio handed the fig to the girl and tickled her under the chin. "Mercedes was my mother's name," he said. "We will call her Soledad Mercedes."

The girl stuck her tongue out at Dionisio and toddled off in the direction of a sleeping pig, suckling the stem of the fig like a nipple.

Dionisio stood up and took Atizania in his arms. "Ciriaco's predictions always come true," he murmured. "But I'm not afraid anymore. A father can't be afraid."

Atizania wept against his shoulder.

Early the next morning, before the priests and the tourists arrived in the pueblo, they baptized Soledad Mercedes in the central patio of the ruins. Ciriaco officiated over the ceremony, wearing necklaces of lapis lazuli, amethyst, and turquoise. Apolonio wore a beaded headband with turkey feathers hanging down the back. Dionisio looked pale and sleepy. He had not closed his eyes all night.

The night before, after dinner, he had worked on his basket until his fingertips were so raw even the wind hurt them. He had blown out his lamp then, and walked across town to the ruins, wanting to lie down on the sacred stones of Mitla and fill his eyes with the falling stars. He'd spent the rest of the night at La Sorpresa, drinking with Matías and his future compadre, Silverio, who was to be Soledad Mercedes's godfather. Near daybreak, he'd climbed the hill that overlooked Mitla and watched the sunrise polish the four domes of the church. Below and beside the church, the ancient ruins crumbled. Then, Dionisio had trudged home to shave and eat his breakfast.

The three of them wore yellow, as was the custom. Dionisio in a freshly ironed yellow guayabera and white pants. Atizania in a yellow huipíl embroidered with peacocks. Soledad Mercedes all wrapped up in the yellow sarape that was her godparents' baptism gift.

The patio was filled with people. The women had daisies in their hair, and the men wore their black shoes. Dionisio imagined that the Mixtec lords and priests had come out of their catacombs to witness the baptism, and he could see them sitting on the steps in front of the palaces in their bright penachos.

The ceremony was a simple one. Ciriaco held a burning censer and Apolonio beside him, a bowl of water and a knife, and together they lifted these implements to the sky. Ciriaco mumbled wordlessly. Apolonio called to the Man of the Thunderbolt and the Mother of the Corn to bless the child with strength and fertility. Next, Ciriaco put the censer on the ground and passed Soledad Mercedes over the smoke four times. Apolonio gave the knife to Silverio, who made an incision on his thumb and another one on his wife's thumb, and each of them painted a cross on the girl's forehead with their blood. Ciriaco washed the blood away with the water and passed Soledad Mercedes over the incense smoke four more times. The girl slept through the whole thing.

After the ceremony, they made a procession to Silverio's and Berta's house, where the fiesta would take place. By the time they reached the house, Dionisio was floating on mezcal and sleeplessness. He saw everything in a tilted light. The people around him looked like the reflections in the crazy mirrors he had seen at the feria in Oaxaca. His own feet had become elongated and were so far down that, for a moment, he thought they'd slipped into the catacombs with the lords and priests. He drank another cup of mezcal and watched Soledad Mercedes playing with the other children. He remembered he had to finish his basket and sent one of Silverio's sons to fetch it for him.

When the boy came back, Dionisio squatted under a mulberry tree and finished stitching the last scorpion into the basket. Atizania brought him a plate of tamales and rice and fed him while he worked. The pink and blue pincers of the other scorpions on the basket snapped at his food.

"Be careful," he told Atizania. "These scorpions are alive. Look! Now they're dancing a jarabe tapatío!"

Atizania rolled her eyes and shook her head. "You need to sleep," she said.

After he had finished eating, Dionisio called for another bottle of mezcal and asked the conjunto to play songs of the Revolution. Silverio brought him the mezcal and poured each of them a generous amount in their tin cups.

"Compadre," said Silverio, squatting beside Dionisio. "This is a fiesta. You're not supposed to be working."

"I have to finish this, compadre," said Dionisio. "No telling when the blindness will strike."

Silverio squinted at Dionisio's basket. "What kind of design is that, compadre?" he asked.

"You like it?" said Dionisio.

Silverio nodded. "Very original, compadre. You could probably get 500 pesos for it in Oaxaca, maybe more if you go during the margarita hour."

Dionisio chuckled. "No, compadre," he said, "this is no turista basket. This is a gift for my little girl. Besides, she's the one who gave me the idea for the design."

"How did she do that, compadre?"

"By standing in front of me, compadre. How else?"

Silverio cracked up laughing. "At least you haven't lost your sense of humor, compadre," he said, holding up his cup. "Here's to a good sense of humor."

"And to Mitla," said Dionisio, hitting his cup against Silverio's.

The two of them were quiet for a moment, Dionisio threading the thin cord of the handles through the bottom of the basket, Silverio listening to "La Adelita." When the song was over, Silverio said:

"Hey, compadre, do you know what Ciriaco told Matías? He said some big changes are coming to Mitla."

"Is that right, compadre?" Dionisio said sarcastically.

"Really!" said Silverio. "It's going to affect everybody, not just you, compadre. It's going to affect all of the Republic. Ciriaco says Mitla is going to sink."

"Ciriaco talks too much," said Dionisio. "Do me a favor, compadre. Tell me if these two handles are the same length. All this mezcal has twisted my vision."

Silverio tucked one of the handles farther into the basket and moved up the knot. "You know what else Ciriaco said?" Silverio whispered. "He said that when you go blind, you're going to be a seer."

"Well, compadre," chuckled Dionisio, "I guess if the mute can talk, the blind can see."

"¡Salud!" said Silverio, and they toasted again.

Dionisio spent the rest of the afternoon singing with the group of men who had gathered around the conjunto. When Atizania came and took his hand and led him to a hammock on the side of Silverio's house, Dionisio lay down obediently and promised to sleep. But his eyes did not want to close. Through the leaves of the tamarind trees he could see the clouds shifting. He saw a hummingbird and a beehive and spotted a kite stuck in the top branches of the mulberry. Then, he caught a flash of green and blue in the corner of his eye. *The scorpions must be following me,* he laughed to himself, but suddenly a parrot perched on a limb above him, and the intensity of the bird's gaze startled Dionisio. He became aware of a deep fear settling in his bones. He had been awake two full days now, swallowing everything he could with his vision, and still the blindness had not come. And now this parrot, which he had never seen in the village before, was looking at him as though to determine his fate. Dionisio reached a hand down and found a pebble and prepared to throw it at the parrot, but a great fatigue came over him, and he could not raise his hand. He could not even keep his eyelids open.

When Dionisio awoke from his siesta, Soledad Mercedes was sleeping beside him, her cheek resting in a pool of her own saliva on his shoulder. Above him, he saw the stars through the dark lattice of the branches. Atizania found him weeping.

Five months passed, and still, Dionisio's eyesight had not left him. Ciriaco explained that it would not happen until Atizania was with child, and Dionisio had taken to relieving his need with the women at La Sorpresa. Atizania did not bother him about it, understanding that in this way, Dionisio avoided fulfilling Ciriaco's prediction. But one Saturday afternoon, upon returning from the market in Oaxaca, Dionisio saw the parrot again. It was perched on the roof of his hut, its blue-green wings bright as semaphores in the dusty afternoon. The neighbors had gathered in the middle of the road to stare at it, none of them more aware than Dionisio that the parrot was the omen of his blindness. Atizania was waiting for him at the door, her scapular hanging over her blouse.

"Tell them to go away," Atizania whispered as Dionisio came in. "They're scaring me, Nicho."

"Come here," said Dionisio behind her. "Don't you realize what that parrot is?"

"I've never seen it before," said Atizania.

"You've never seen me blind, either," he said, leading her to the back of the hut.

"Nicho, it's not a good idea," she said.

He stripped her slowly, amazed at the different shades of her body, the deep bronze of her arms and legs, the pink-gold of her breasts and buttocks. He took her in his favorite way. When his moment came, he clenched his jaw to keep from waking Soledad Mercedes.

On Monday, while guiding three Canadian ladies through the ruins, Dionisio's sombrero was blown off by the wind. He chased after it, caught it before it tumbled into the churchyard, and pushed it down on his head. A twig had gotten hooked on the brim of the sombrero and was dangling over his forehead. He was just about to pull it off, when he realized that the twig was a scorpion's tail, arching down to sting him between the eyebrows. The last thing Dionisio saw before the sight drained out of his eyes was the crucifix on one of the cupolas of the church.

The Last Rite

For sixty of her ninety-two years, Estrella González had been singing in her garden every evening before retiring. After her third prayer to the sun at sunset, she would roam among the herbs for a while, deepening the furrows around them, pinching off the dead leaves, pronouncing each of their names in Latin, and invoking their essences to come out of the ground to revitalize her healing powers. Then she would sing.

But in this October twilight, she felt tired again. She had already talked to the plants and fed the parrot and the rooster, but she still had to take Malinche, her mule, her nightly medicine. The poor mule was getting old now, her eyes almost completely shrouded in cataracts, but she knew that Estrella still depended on her to carry her up and down the foothills to the village, and, once a year, to San Cristóbal de las Casas, for the yearly curandera gathering. As Estrella approached her singing place—a huge slab of lodestone that she had unearthed under the Adobe Room—she heard the parrot insulting the rooster inside the hut:

"¡Pinche gallo! Go to hell! Go to hell!"

Estrella shook her head and chuckled at her eccentric family of animals. The black stone rocked with her weight as she sat down. She dug her hand between her breasts and pulled out the small reed flute that she kept on a string. Her hand lingered a moment over the left nipple, now swollen more than ever before. She had stopped fomenting the blisters, and sometimes, especially on amethyst nights like this one with the October moon rising in Libra, she regretted knowing her destiny.

"Ay, Madre," she sighed, "I *am* getting too old, just like my Malinche." She could feel the tears creeping into her eyes like foxes, but tonight she would not weep; she could not forget who she was. "Estrella González!" she called aloud, "where is your faith?"

She put the flute to her lips, closing her eyes so that the music would run out of her like water, so that all she could see were the swirling stars at the back of her head. When she sang, her voice carried with it the baying of the foxes.

> *"Salías del templo un día, Llorona,*
> *cuando al pasar yo te vi.*
> *Hermoso huipil llevabas, Llorona,*
> *que la virgen te creí."*

The Ballad of La Llorona gave her the most comfort on these long nights of waiting for it reminded her of Malintzin, mother of La Raza, and of Tonantzin and Coatlicue, mothers of the Earth and of the Night—the immortal memories in her blood. In six months, she would perform the greatest, the most difficult, of all her experiments, and she needed the Mothers to lend her more power.

> *"Ay de mí, Llorona,*
> *Llorona de ayer y hoy.*
> *Ayer maravilla fui, Llorona,*
> *y ahora ni sombra soy."*

Her voice faltered now, in the middle of the song, and her notes on the flute were more like the whimpers of an old, indomitable longing. The music stopped, and she got up heavily, pushing herself off the lodestone with a grunt.

"Six months," she mumbled, walking towards her hut, barely lifting her feet from the ground. She stroked the thunderbird on the sarape that served as her door and remembered that she had to set out the jugs. It was going to rain later, and she needed to collect the rainwater for her altar.

The hut felt cold. She hurried lighting the fire, then placed a kettle of water to boil for her tea. She would have the palo azul bark to strengthen her kidneys, orange blossoms to bring sleep, and cinnamon for spice.

"Strong kidneys give you a long life," she told the parrot, who had heard it all before and just preened under his turquoise-colored wings. "It's a wonder you haven't died with all the mezcal you drink!" she scolded.

"Go to hell!" the parrot squawked, "go to hell!"

She tried to get the rooster to come out from behind the trunk, but he had still not recovered from her last experiment. He refused to crow in the mornings, and he didn't trust anything that she gave him to eat or drink. "¡Pinche gallo!" she said. The parrot echoed her curse.

Estrella wasn't in the mood for her nightly ritual. She had become so vain since her ninetieth birthday and had taken to smearing her body every night with a cream that she made herself, grinding the herbs in the molcajete and letting them steep in a bowl of grease that hardened in the two hours that it took to do her studying. But she didn't feel strong enough to study tonight, much less to do any grinding. What if she used the fish oil that she reserved only for the Mothers' work?

"Just this once," she muttered. Surely there would be no harm if she just used a drop or two to ease the wrinkles in her face. She did feel so tired, and the thought of making anything other than her tea exhausted her even more. *Yes,* she thought, *just a drop or two can't hurt.*

She passed through another sarape at the back of the hut and into the Adobe Room. The smell of copal permeated her bones, and she knew that invisible eyes watched her in the penumbra as she made the sign of the five points before the altar.

"Madres," she whispered to the wood, paper, and clay figures on the altar, "guardians of this room and its implements, I beg you to forgive me for taking of this oil to soothe my withered flesh." She took a copper bowl that hung from a nail on the wall and poured into it a few drops of dark oil that gleamed like the melted wax of the candles. The smell of seaweed and fish cloyed her nostrils as she rubbed the first drop on her forehead. When she came out into the main room, her eyes were stung by the bright flames of the fire. She noticed that her water was boiling and took a few pieces of bark, a handful of dry petals, and a strip of cinnamon from their respective jars and dropped everything into the kettle.

As she removed her blouse, her skirts, she hummed another tune of *La Llorona*; it was a tremulous humming filled suddenly with the memory of her only child, a memory that she did not allow herself to indulge in, for she was too old and had learned too much to regret anything. But the memory stayed, and she tried to defend herself against its accusations.

The little girl was dying in her care. Estrella's Learning took her away from the hut for days, and she would forget that the child was waiting for her, eating dirt, and playing in chicken droppings. Estrella had not wanted to have a child. She had simply been experimenting with the egg and had ended up using her body as the laboratory. Her pregnancy had not been the surprising thing; even at seventy she had been fertile, thanks to her teas. The truth is, she didn't expect the egg to have the effect that it did on the young man. He had just come to deliver the wood the villagers sent her once a week, and Estrella had offered him breakfast. The egg looked darker than he was accustomed to, but it was good, he said, especially with that spicy salsa on top. The next thing Estrella knew, the young man was on top of her, poking under her skirts. She had laughed through the whole thing and for weeks afterwards congratulated herself on the potent aphrodisiac she had created. And then her blood stopped. Her old breasts filled with milk.

She could have stopped the child. Could have taken toloache or punched herself in the belly, but she had wanted to see the results of the experiment. Maybe it would not be a child at all, but a monster born of an inhuman seed, a creature to dissect and investigate. But it had turned out to be human, after all. A girl with too much sugar in her blood.

Just after the girl's third birthday, the parrot brought her the rumor of a prediction in Mitla, an old Zapotec ghost town more popular with the tourists than the ghosts. The town bordered the ancient Zapotec and Mixtec catacombs, three days north of La Subida. The prediction had been made by the same curandero whom Estrella had ousted from La Subida sixty years before. It was in this way that fate always worked for Estrella González. And so Malinche, the mule, took them north to Mitla to leave the girl in the ruins where some turista would probably find her.

Estrella never expected to see the girl again, but thirteen years later she appeared, as miraculously as the Virgin whose name she'd been given, one afternoon in Estrella's garden, seeking a potion to give death to her own child. Estrella had never told the girl the truth. The truth was *her* burden. The girl had other crosses to carry.

"Y aunque la vida me cueste, Llorona,
no dejaré de quererte."

Estrella sang softly, her head swaying with each word as she uncoiled her long braids. Once her hair was loosened and hung down her back, she stepped over to the fire and knelt down. Taking the copper bowl from the table, she held it over the flames, rotating it slowly between her palms. The fire licked at her bracelets as it warmed the dark green oil. She felt her pubic hair and her armpits grow damp. On his perch, the parrot rustled his wings at her, nearly losing his balance in the heat of the room.

The oil released a strong, salty odor, and Estrella felt herself getting dizzy as she set the bowl down next to her on the dirt floor. Rivulets of sweat ran down the middle of her spine and between her breasts. Eyes closed, she dipped three fingers of each hand into the bowl. She rubbed the warm oil over the loose skin of her neck and could hear herself singing silently:

"Dicen que no tengo duelo, Llorona,
porque no me ven llorar.
Hay muertos que no hacen ruido, Llorona,
y es más grande su penar."

As she continued to wet her fingers in the oil, dabbing it behind her earlobes, in the hollow of her throat, on each nipple, under the arms, and on the inside of each wrist and knee, she felt her body move from side to side in a rhythmic swaying that removed her fatigue. Head hanging back, hair trailing in the dirt, she started speaking her name in one of the first old languages that she had learned, the words ululating out of her throat:

" *'Ek'etik! 'Ek'etik! 'Ek'etik!*"

Even with her eyes shut, she could see the room circling about her. The fire lapped at her in huge, roaring flames, and she realized that her body had become very small, that she stood beneath a great cloud of flames, the Scorpion's nest; her arms reached up to it, her fingers clawing the brilliant air. She could feel herself about to perform the Dance of the Scorpion Cross, the old fertility dance.

"*Tsek*, Scorpio!" she called, looking up at the fire cloud as the Scorpion arched its giant tail and stung her skull with its white light.

"*Kurus'ek!*" she cried, facing north as the Scorpion's tail injected the light into her lungs and heart. Fire shot down through her spine and formed a pillar of light in her body. Slowly, the Scorpion's great pincers pierced her belly.

"*Sakubee ek'*!" she wailed, facing east, "*Yek' uljch' ultatik!*" She faced west. The pincers gripped her ovaries, and the Cross of the Scorpion burned inside her as she whirled around the room. At the end of the dance, she cupped her breasts in her hands and milked the light out of her body.

When she awoke two hours later, she found herself lying naked on the ground next to the smoldering logs. The kettle she had filled with water had turned over, drenching the fish skulls that she used as a border for her hearth. At first she did not remember the Dance of the Scorpion Cross. Her head throbbed, and her whole body felt hot and cold at the same time. Her lips were covered with sand, and she felt thirsty. She wiped her mouth with the back of her hand, closing her eyes as she tried to recall how much of the mezcal she had imbibed, cursing silently at her self-indulgence. She heard rain pattering on the tin roof.

"But I ran *out* of mezcal!" she cried out, sitting up quickly. The mezcal jug had been empty for days now, just like the water jugs she had forgotten to set out. She remembered she had used the oil of the Mothers.

"¡Santa Madre!" she cried again as the image of the tail and pincers filtered out of her memory. How could she have been so stupid? This was a time of preparation. She could not allow the old rituals to mount her until she was stronger. If only she had made her usual cream. She got to her knees groggily, the pain slicing through her head with each movement, but now she welcomed that pain and her fever and thirst, as well. Her punishments for being such a lazy weakling, such a lazy, crazy vieja!

"Loca! Loca!" screeched the parrot.

Estrella felt like poisoning the bird. She groped around for her clothes and found one of her skirts near the table. She threw it over her head and pulled it down to her waist, wincing as the coarse fabric grazed her breasts. There! She had gone and infected the nipple again, lying in that dirt. Well, that's what she deserved for her foolishness. She lumbered up the ladder to the platform where she kept her most precious things: her books, the water jugs, and her morral—the snakeskin medicine bag that held the sacred earth and thorns from the hill of Tepeyac.

It took her a long time to carry down all the jugs, and by the time she finished, the rain had abated. Her efforts had been useless. The rain would stop any minute, and it would not rain again for months. Her thirst became unbearable, and she knew that she had better allow herself at least a few drops of water, otherwise her fever would increase, and she would not be able to get up in the morning. She leaned against the hut, opened her mouth, and let the drizzle cool her parched tongue. She would not let the vision of the Scorpion Cross surface again, but standing out here, she could not help but contrast the burning light and the chilly darkness. Malinche brayed once, reminding Estrella that she still had to make the salve that ate at the mule's cataracts.

Later, as she lay exhausted in her hammock, watching the Milky Way through the hole in the roof, she invoked the spirit of La Gran María, mother of the First Name, whom she called upon only when the doubts swelled like goiters. She had been so weak lately, given to fits of rage and despair and outright sensuality. Just last year, she'd gathered all her herbs in a basket and cast them into the bay, and then, to the embarrassment of the villagers, she had stripped herself like a prostitute and waded into the sea, a fat old woman having a tantrum because her experiments weren't giving her the results she wanted. Since then, her cures hadn't been the same. The healings had become monotonous, and she found herself doubting her abilities more and more.

Tonight, she needed La Gran María to fortify her faith for this most vital of all her experiments. In her sixty years of experimentation, she had never inseminated anything other than chickens and ducks. If she allowed the doubts to root inside her, the egg would rot, and the scorpion would kill her. The experiment for which she had been preparing her entire life, her mission as a curandera, would fail. If she failed, the one the Mothers were waiting for would not be born. Estrella González could have no doubts. Everything was ready. All she had to do was wait for the stranger who would call at her house in six months, a young man of the new breed bringing her word of another religion. After feeding him well and extracting his seed, Estrella would send him to her daughter in Mitla. Thus, the experiment would begin, and it would end on the night of the insemination.

"Six months," she sighed.

"Six months," the parrot repeated.

Just before her eyelids closed, Estrella heard the rooster come out of his hiding place behind the trunk, his talons scratching at the floor as he scurried out to the garden. When the rooster crowed, she knew that La Gran María was with her, a blood-fresh presence in the room.

"Madre," she spoke, "I know that the insemination will be my last rite; that, once it is finished, I will shed this old skin, and with it will go all my power as well as my illness. But will it work, Madre? Will the egg carry the memories?"

The egg is the name, Estrella González, the mother of the First Name answered. *Just as La Gran María evokes the gramarye of our kind, the name you choose must evoke the memories. If the ritual does not work, it will be because you have chosen the wrong name.*

The rooster crowed again, and Estrella González took her flute out and played another tune of the *Ballad of La Llorona.*

Facing the Mariachis

Mercedes woke up screaming again. Her husband sat up in the bed and reached for his glasses and his cigarette case. He struck a match, held it in front of her face for a moment, then lit a cigarette.

"Is this one of your customs?" he asked in his gringo-like Spanish.

Mercedes buried her face in her hands. She was afraid, not just because of the dream, but because she knew he was getting tired of all this nonsense and mystery. They had been on their honeymoon for only a week, and she had already made the same scandal three times.

"Talk to me Mercedes," he said. "Tell me what the problem is. Let me help you."

Mercedes shook her head and would not look at him. "I hope the man in the office didn't hear me *this* time," she said, staring down at the sheet.

"Who cares about that?" he said. "The important thing is that you tell me what's wrong. This didn't happen before we were married. Are you unhappy?"

"¡Ay, José!" she said, "how many times do I have to tell you that I'm happy? It has nothing to do with you or with us."

"What is it, then?"

The thick smoke of American tobacco hung over the bed like a mosquito net.

"I have to go to confession tomorrow," she said. "There's something in my soul that doesn't let me sleep in peace."

"Do you know what it is?"

Mercedes covered her mouth with her hand and shook her head again.

"Then how are you going to confess it, Mercedes?"

She shrugged. "Sins come out in the confessional," she said. He tried to hold her, but she pulled away.

The next morning while José ate breakfast in the courtyard of the hotel, Mercedes hurried to the Basilica of the Virgin of Solitude, La Soledad, the miraculous patroness of Oaxaca. At the entrance to the cathedral, Mercedes got on her hands and knees and crawled up to the altar beside an Indian woman whose knees bled.

"Help me, Señora," she muttered once she knelt at the communion banister below the Virgin's shrine. "I'm so afraid he'll divorce me when he finds out. But I have to tell him the truth. Guide me, Virgencita, por favor! Give me courage."

The slanted eyes of La Soledad looked down at Mercedes, and Mercedes took her rosary from her purse and prayed a Padre Nuestro and the first decade of Hail Mary. *Go to the Man of the Thunderbolt*, she heard the Virgin say, *it is his help you need, not mine*.

Still on her knees, Mercedes crept to the room in the basilica where a black Christ, known to the people as El Señor del Rayo, hung on a black cross, his shrine crammed with milagros and daisies and lilies of the valley. Mercedes made the sign of the cross.

"Señor," she whispered, "give me the light and the strength of the thunderbolt. If you help me to tell him the truth, and if you help him to understand it, I promise I will return in one year to baptize this child here in your shrine.

"Padre Nuestro que estás en el cielo . . ." she prayed, watching the caretaker of the church replace the expired candles at the foot of the crucifix. She felt the beads passing under her fingers as she mumbled the rest of the rosary, the smell of the melted wax guiding her back to the adobe room in La Subida where her deepest secret had been conceived.

* * *

Estrella González handed her a cup of tea that was so bitter it numbed Mercedes's tongue and made the rest of her body languid as a sponge. La Vieja told her to undress and to lie down on the straw mat with her knees bent. The tea gave her a strange kind of fever; her eyes burned and her ears felt like ovens. She could barely discern what Estrella González was doing through the burning film over her eyes and the glare of all those candles. She had seen a large, black egg on La Vieja's altar, and now Estrella González was holding the egg over Mercedes's face, speaking in a language that Mercedes did not recognize. She laid the egg between Mercedes's breasts.

" 'Ek'etik!" La Vieja called to the dark air. "Tsek! Kurus'ek!"

Mercedes watched La Vieja approach her altar, take a scorpion from an earthen bowl, and place the scorpion under her tongue. Mercedes had heard the rumors about La Vieja's immunity to the scorpion poison; it was said that, in fact, her powers came from that poison and that was what made Estrella González the most potent bruja-curandera in all of México; but Mercedes had never imagined that she would witness such a thing. She watched as the poison shocked the old woman's body into a convulsive dance. Her eyes became red flames. Her skin shone as though wires of lightning ran in her veins. She spit the carcass of the scorpion on the floor, and she shrieked. Mercedes felt a sudden nausea welling up, a mixture of fear and the bitter tea boiling in her stomach.

She closed her eyes, and when she reopened them, Estrella González was bending over her, taking the black egg apart in two perfect halves. She threw the top half aside; a gray-blue substance that smelled of starch steamed in the bottom half. The bruja put a drop of this thick, hot liquid on Mercedes's tongue; Mercedes felt her nipples harden, her genitals grow moist.

"Yo soy el recuerdo y el destino," Estrella González uttered in Spanish. "I am the memory and the destiny. El huevo y la culebra. The egg and the snake."

She placed another drop of the substance on each of Mercedes's nipples. Mercedes felt her hips moving as if José were on top of her. Her belly undulated to the rhythm of La Vieja's chant:

"Tu vientre será la piñata. La piñata cargará el recuerdo. Cuando se quiebre la piñata, el recuerdo será el destino de la que viene."

Now, Estrella González tipped the egg over Mercedes's belly and let a fat drop of the substance fill her navel. Mercedes felt rays of fire radiate through her womb, melting her genitals. Even her lungs burned. Her tongue was like a live coal. The bruja cupped the claw of her hand over Mercedes's navel, digging her cracked nails into the flesh, and repeated the chant:

"Your womb shall be the piñata. The piñata shall carry the memory. When the piñata breaks, the memory will be the destiny of she who comes."

The fire had spread down into her legs and feet. Mercedes raised her knees parallel to her ribs. She needed air. She needed air to stream through all the holes in her body and cool the hot contractions in her womb.

Estrella González poured what was left in the egg into her own mouth. She lowered her head between Mercedes's thighs, pressed her lips below the nest of black hair, and spit the starchy substance into Mercedes. Mercedes shuddered as she had never shuddered with José.

When Mercedes awoke from the ritual the fever was gone. She had a headache and a dull pain around her navel, but she could sit up on the petate and get herself dressed. She noticed they were in the main room of the hut, now, instead of the adobe room where the ritual had taken place. Estrella González was clapping tortillas into shape, and the room was filled with the aroma of nixtamal.

"She will be born on the year that begins on the flower day, the day called Xochitl," the old woman said, placing a raw tortilla on the griddle.

Mercedes buttoned up her blouse. She was hungry and embarrassed at having climaxed in La Vieja's mouth during the ritual.

"Do you know what name you are going to give her?" Estrella González asked. She laid another tortilla on the comal.

"No, mi vieja. I haven't thought about it." Deep inside her, Mercedes did not really believe that La Vieja's magic had impregnated her.

"I have just told you the name," said La Vieja.

Mercedes replayed what the old woman had said. "You mean Xochitl?" she asked.

"Only by seeding the new world with the old names will the memories come back," said Estrella González.

"I'm sorry, mi vieja. I don't understand you."

La Vieja turned the tortillas to let them cook on the other side. Mercedes felt saliva gathering under her tongue. She braided her hair as La Vieja spoke.

"Five hundred years ago, the name Mercedes and the religious order from whence that name comes did not exist in our language or our culture. Then, *they* came. Took our gods and our land away. Changed our language and our ways. But the memories stayed, even though you do not remember them, and even after 500 years of silence, the memories are still alive."

She took the tortillas off the comal and wrapped them in a flour sack.

"The one inside you will be a voice in the new generation, Mercedes. If she does not have an old name, the new world will devour her. She will never bloom if the memories are buried. With a name like Xochitl, she will find it more difficult to forget. Now come. It is time to eat."

* * *

Mercedes found José waiting for her on a bench in the zócalo, shading a bunch of gardenias under his Panama hat. Mercedes swallowed back her fear and smiled at him as she took the fragrant flowers.

"¿Ya estás mejor?" he asked after kissing her lightly on the mouth.

She nodded and touched the gardenias to her nose.

"You won't have any more nightmares?"

"José," she said so softly it sounded like her shadow had spoken. "I have to tell you something. I've prayed, and the Man of the Thunderbolt has answered me. I couldn't ask for your forgiveness beforehand, but the Señor del Rayo said you would understand. He said Chicanos are different from Mexicans; your minds are more open than ours, he said."

José stood up, took her hand, and led her to one of the open-air cafes that bordered the plaza. When the waitress appeared, he ordered two mezcal margaritas for himself. Mercedes asked for black coffee. She waved away the little vendor girls who passed with Chiclets and canastas and the boys who wanted to shine their shoes. She began her confession after the waitress had set their order on the table.

"For three nights," she started, looking down at the coffee, "I've dreamt that I'm standing before a firing squad, my head covered up in a black sack."

José finished the first margarita in one swallow.

"In the dream, perhaps in real life, I know I deserve to be shot for what I've done, but still, I want to plead for my life, or for another form of death, at least, but I have a gag on my mouth and cannot speak. Then, I hear a voice shout ¡*Fuego*! The bullets explode, and my belly bursts into flames. That's when I wake up screaming."

José drank his second margarita. "What have you done?" he asked.

"You're not going to like this," she said.

"I'm a man," he said and held up two fingers to the waitress. Again, Mercedes waited for the waitress to bring his margaritas. She sipped her coffee and watched her husband's face. He traced the crust of salt on one of the glasses.

"I fought in Viet Nam, Mercedes. Nothing you could say could be worse than what I lived in that war."

Mercedes was beginning to feel dizzy. She had neglected to eat breakfast, and now her blood was craving sugar. She dipped half her spoon into the sugar bowl and stirred it into the tepid coffee.

"When I was fourteen our curandero's assistant, Apolonio . . . raped me in my father's cornfield," she confessed. "I was too afraid and too ashamed to tell anybody, so I kept it a secret and in that way gave him license to do it to me again. Seeing that no punishment came to him, he did it several times, and he started the rumor that I made eyes at him, and that I appeared to him in his dreams in the form of a cow begging him to take my milk. When I became pregnant, my mother forced me to tell her who the father was, but she didn't believe that Apolonio had raped me. She, too, had heard the rumors that I flirted with Apolonio, and as punishment, she made me marry him."

She drank the sweetened coffee, grimacing at the taste, at the memory of Apolonio.

"He was so disgusting, chasing after me all the time, too sick with his lust to understand that it was wrong to have relations with a pregnant girl. I was only fourteen years old. My body hadn't even finished forming yet."

Mercedes's voice trembled. José stroked her hand.

"Apolonio came from a cursed family. Each generation bred a new sickness into the blood. His parents were brother and sister, and his family had been doing that for a long time. With my diabetes and Apolonio's bad blood, never mind his brutality, I didn't expect the baby to be normal. But I *never* suspected the monster that came out of my body."

Mercedes squeezed her eyes shut and saw again the watermelon-shaped head, the rheumy eyes on either side of it. Heard again that horrible cat-like howl that filled the village like the music of death.

"Even Apolonio could see that there was something terribly wrong with the child, that he was an aberration, a thing of the devil. The priest stopped by to bless the child and ended up excommunicating us instead, saying that God had punished us for practicing our heathen beliefs. The whole village turned against us, except my father. It was my father who suggested that I seek the help of Estrella González, the wise woman of La Subida. He said that she would be able to advise me better than anybody and perhaps even help me release the boy's soul from that tortured little body."

Mercedes looked up at José. "If you had seen him, José. Those eyes of his caked with that yellow mucus that hardened around his eyelids and made him scratch so hard he drew blood and howled even louder than he normally did. If you had seen the way he beat his head on the floor giving himself bruises and bumps that only deformed his face even more than it already was. And the way he convulsed when Apolonio kicked him in the stomach to make him stop howling. I was going crazy. I knew I had to listen to my father.

"I walked all the way to La Subida. It took me four days to get there and another day just to find the wise woman's house in that labyrinth of prickly pears. She didn't want to help me at first. Said she was a curandera, not an hechicera, that she had the power to heal, not to hurt. When I told her that she would be healing the boy's soul by releasing him from that cursed body, she told me to go back home and bring the boy to her, but I think she had already decided to help me because when I returned, she had the poison ready."

"She poisoned him?" José said.

Mercedes shook her head. "I did," she answered.

José lit a cigarette and watched a mariachi band that was walking across the zócalo.

"Is that all?" José said, keeping his gaze on the mariachis.

"I had another problem," Mercedes went on. "As soon as Apolonio recuperated from the shock of that monster, or forgot how it had come into being, he started chasing after me again. It didn't scare him at all when I threatened him with the machete. In fact, that made his lust grow, and he would take it out and rub himself in front of me and let it squirt on the floor. I went back to Estrella González, and she gave me some powders to make him impotent. But you see, I was just fifteen and already had a dead son. I could see a whole family of monsters coming out of my womb. I didn't trust those powders. I begged Estrella González to give me something stronger, an extract like the one she'd made for the boy."

The Americans at the table beside them had flagged down the mariachis, and Mercedes did not feel like raising her voice over

"Cielito lindo." José asked for another margarita; Mercedes ordered orange juice. She could see that José was getting nervous. His eyebrows had started to twitch.

The Americans listened politely to "Cielito lindo" and "De colores." Then they clapped, paid the musicians, and went back to talking in English. The mariachis wandered down to the far end of the cafe.

Mercedes swallowed some juice and prepared herself for the worst part of the confession, imploring the Man of the Thunderbolt to help her finish what she had started. "I know this will be hard . . ."

José held up both his hands. "Wait!" he said. "If you're going to tell me that you poisoned that animal you had to marry, if that's the sin you had to confess, we don't have a problem, mi amor. Protecting yourself isn't a sin. And it would have been more cruel to let that boy live. In the United States we call that kind of death *euthanasia*."

"I didn't know there was a word for it," Mercedes said, her eyes starting to sting.

"Well, there is, and it is *not* a sin. So stop punishing yourself. I love you, Mercedes. I can't blame you for what you had to do." He stroked her face with the back of his hand and her tears spilled over his fingers.

"José," she murmured, "are you sure?" The words felt like thorns in her throat.

"¡Música!" José yelled to the mariachis, waving his hat to get their attention. Mercedes held her breath. She could not tell him now that poisoning Apolonio and the boy was just the background to her real secret. She could not tell him that, as payment for the wise woman's potions, she had agreed to let Estrella González plant a child inside her with her magic. A child she had not believed would take root. A child that now fed herself on Mercedes's blood.

On the day that the stranger who will be your second husband proposes to you, La vieja had said fifteen years ago as Mercedes walked out of her hut with Apolonio's poison, *I will come to you in Mitla and bring you some herbs to prepare your body.*

Prepare my body for what, mi vieja?

For you to repay me for my infusions. Todo se paga en la vida, Mercedes. Everything must be paid for in life.

"What song do you want to hear?" José asked her once the mariachis were gathered before them.

Mercedes could not speak. She was dizzy again. The orange

juice and the coffee bubbled like acid in her stomach. The thorns in her throat had become nails. José asked for the "Corrido de Gregorio Cortez," but the mariachis didn't know it.

"That's a corrido from the north, ¿que no? From Texas, isn't it?" said the man on the guitarrón.

"Our specialty is 'El niño perdido,' " said one of the trumpeters. "Would you like to hear it?"

"Bueno, pues," said José, throwing his legs up on an empty chair and his arm around Mercedes. He gestured to the waitress to bring another round.

The two trumpeters walked to the back of the arcade while the guitars, the violins, and the guitarrón started to play. There were no words to the music; the melody itself formed the story of a lost boy crying to be found. The strings were the voices that called out to him; the keening of the distant trumpets was the lost boy's response.

Mercedes did not want to hear this counterpoint. Each time the horns blew, a dog in the plaza howled, and in that howling, Mercedes heard the wails of her dead son, a sound that was buried in the marrow of her bones. She realized then that she was reliving the dream. Lined up before her in their black suits the mariachis were her executioners and the bullets were the wailing notes of the trumpet, growing louder as the lost boy drew closer, blasting her with the memory of her son.

He had been quiet for fifteen years, and now that another body was forming inside her, his spirit was trying to scream its way back into her womb. "The memories are still alive," Estrella González had said. "Todo se paga en la vida." Mercedes felt her eyes blow open like balloons. She knew there was no way to poison a spirit. Or a memory.

"¿Les gustó?" the guitarrón man asked them when the piece was finished.

"¡Fantástico!" said José, and he promised to buy them each a shot of mezcal if they would play "El niño perdido" one more time.

"Claro que sí, con mucho gusto," said the trumpeter.

"We dedicate it to the señora," said one of the others.